Benedictus de Spinoza, William Hale-White, Amelia H. Stirling

Tractatus de Intellectus Emendatione

et de via, qua optime in veram rerum cognitionem dirigitur

Benedictus de Spinoza, William Hale-White, Amelia H. Stirling

Tractatus de Intellectus Emendatione
et de via, qua optime in veram rerum cognitionem dirigitur

ISBN/EAN: 9783337367541

Printed in Europe, USA, Canada, Australia, Japan

Cover: Foto ©Andreas Hilbeck / pixelio.de

More available books at **www.hansebooks.com**

TRACTATUS
DE INTELLECTUS
EMENDATIONE

ET DE VIA, QUA OPTIME IN VERAM
RERUM COGNITIONEM DIRIGITUR

TRANSLATED FROM THE LATIN
OF BENEDICT DE SPINOZA
BY W. HALE WHITE. TRANS-
LATION REVISED BY AMELIA
HUTCHISON STIRLING M.A. (EDIN.)

London
T FISHER UNWIN
MDCCCXCV

PREFACE.

—◆—

THE *Tractatus de Intellectus Emendatione*, written probably before Spinoza was thirty years old, is so important not only historically, as showing how gradually and consecutively what he had to tell the world was revealed to him, but for its own intrinsic worth, that no excuse is necessary for the attempt to translate and explain it.

It was first published in the *Opera Posthuma* in 1677, but we do not know what MS. the editors had before them. They describe it in the general preface as "one of the earlier works of our Philosopher, as the style and thoughts both testify." [1] Prefixed to the Treatise there is also a "Notice to the Reader," to the following effect :—

"The Treatise concerning the Amendment of the Intellect, which we here present to you, kind reader, incomplete, was written many years ago by

[1] We know that it was written in Latin, for the Preface to the *Opera Posthuma*, expressly states that they were written in Latin with the exception of a few letters. (See also Bruder, vol. i. p. xxiv.)

the author. He always had it in his mind to finish
it. Hindered, however, by other work, and at
length snatched away by death, he could not bring
it to the desired conclusion. Since, however, it
contains much that is remarkable and useful, which,
we do not doubt, will be not a little profitable to
the sincere inquirer after truth, we were unwilling
to deprive you of it. In order, further, that you
may not be disinclined to pardon much obscurity,
and even ruggedness and want of polish which here
and there appear in it, we have desired also to warn
you of these, that you might not be unprepared.
Farewell."

In a letter from Spinoza to Oldenburg, undated,
but in reply to one from Oldenburg, dated October,
1661. Spinoza says : "As to your new question, in
what manner things began to be, and what is the
bond of dependence between them and the first
cause ; on this subject, and also concerning the
emendation of the Intellect, I have written a complete little Treatise, and am at present busy in
copying and correcting it. But sometimes I stay
my hand, for as yet I cannot make up my mind
about publishing the work. I fear lest the theo-
logians of our day, with their customary rancour,
should attack me, who have such an utter horror of
quarrels. On this point I will look for your advice,
and in order that you may know what is contained
in this work of mine, which may serve for a
stumbling-block to these raisers of tumults, I tell
you that many attributes which by these theo-
logians and by all—at least who are known to me

—are assigned to God, I consider as things created (*tanquam creaturas*) ; and, on the other hand, other things considered by them on account of their prejudices as things created, I contend are attributes of God misunderstood by them. Also that I should not separate God from Nature in such a way as all have done with whom I am acquainted."

Oldenburg asked Spinoza to publish the treatise, and at any rate, if he could not, to send an abstract of it. Spinoza in reply, after telling Oldenburg about the *Descartes* which was about to see the light, proceeds as follows :

"At this opportunity, some perchance will be found occupying the foremost positions in my country who will desire to see other things which I have written and acknowledge for my own, and they will take care that I may be enabled to make them common property without any danger of inconvenience. If this should so turn out, I do not doubt that there are certain things which I may immediately publish : but if it should not so turn out, I will rather be silent than intrude my opinions on men, when my country opposes, and so render them hostile to me. I pray, therefore, my honoured friend, that you will not be vexed at having to wait a little longer. You shall then receive from me either the Treatise printed, or the abstract for which you ask."

Now it is quite clear that the *Treatise*, as we have it, does not correspond to the Treatise which Spinoza distinctly said he *had completed* in 1661. There is no discussion of the question "in what manner things began to be," nor of the "bond of dependence between them and the first cause," nor of the attributes of God, nor of the separation of God from Nature, nor is there anything which would have been likely to excite the special theological hostility so much dreaded. Furthermore, not only does the *Treatise* break off abruptly, but there are numerous gaps in it, and references to passages which no longer exist. Examples of these can be found on pp. 4, 7, 22, 57. There is the note to p. 13—*Hic aliquando prolixius agam de experientia, et empiricorum et recentium philosophorum procedendi methodum examinabo ;* a promise which was never performed. It is to be observed that in this last case Spinoza does not say that he has actually written down his criticism on the empirical philosophy. What he intends to write *aliquando* will nevertheless form a part of the Treatise.

Once more, not only is the style of the Treatise singularly rough, but the connection between the different parts is difficult. It is not easy to fix a definite meaning on many portions of it, but it is still less easy to see how some portions hang together ; and I am by no means sure that each of the parts of the rest of the Treatise really follows from what precedes.

It is not unlikely, therefore—I do not say that it is certain—that the MS. of the Treatise which was used by the editors of the Posthumous Works was not the MS. to which Spinoza refers in the Oldenburg correspondence, but merely an incomplete first draft of it. At any rate, if we accept the printed

Treatise as the *integrum opusculum*, the difficulties are insurmountable.

I propose now to set forth the principal doctrines of this little book, and to make a few remarks thereon ; but I may observe that it is almost impossible to obtain any explanation of it in detail from Spinoza's commentators. The mass of literature which includes it with Spinoza's other works is very great ; but, with the exception of Sir F. Pollock, nearly all the writers content themselves with an account of what they call Spinosism, and leave particular passages untouched.

First of all, it will be better to explain the meaning of some of the terms used. It may be observed generally that Spinoza, and he is not singular in this respect, often uses one word to cover several distinct ideas. We find it almost impossible to understand how so many meanings could have been shut up into one expression, although we ourselves continually employ one word in order to designate what is not one. Habit blinds us to our inaccuracy, and yet, when we have learned to specialise, we cannot imagine how the entities newly named could have collapsed under a single term. As an example in Spinoza there is the word *idea*.

The idea is the mental correlate of the external object ; or, rather, the idea and the object are the same thing conceived under two different attributes. Soul and body are not utterly diverse entities, but the same thing, the soul being the idea of the body.

Secondly, the word is used for accurate knowledge. The mathematician is said by Spinoza to possess an idea of proportionality if he understands a proposition in Euclid. In this sense, when we know the chemical composition of iron rust, we have an idea of it, which we cannot be said to have if we simply know that rust is red and comes with damp. The idea is the result of thought, and, in fact, *cogitatio* is used for *idea*.

The exposition of this doctrine must be sought in the *Ethic*.

Thirdly, the *idea* of the imagination contrasted with "idea" as just defined stands for mere picture, something which may be true or false, and may disappear altogether with increase of knowledge.

Essence is that which makes a thing what it is. We are said to know *per essentiam* when we see that if two lines are parallel to a third they are parallel to one another. When I know the essence of the soul—*i.e.*, what soul means or is—I understand it to be united to the body.

Objective essence, again, answers to idea in its second sense, and to possess the objective essence of anything means certainty. It is hardly necessary to repeat what has been said elsewhere, that "objective" has precisely the reverse meaning of that attached to it now, and that Spinoza understands by it that which has been *ob*jected, or the mental representation.

Formal means what we should now call objective ; that which has actuality or form. Descartes talks of " actual or formal " reality.

The end of the Treatise is not so much speculative as moral. The purpose of the quest is a joy which shall be permanent, and consequently the discovery of the highest good. It never occurs here or elsewhere to Spinoza that all is vanity, and his freedom from doubt and mental paralysis is the more singular, seeing that he was without any of the customary supports provided by religion, and was also very nearly solitary in his denial of them. The same healthy faith is found in Bruno, between whom and Spinoza there is considerable parallelism, and, indeed, in both of them, Bruno especially there is an ecstatic delight not to be surpassed by that of the most credulous saint, but resting on a far surer basis. This is a significant fact for modern times. The rapture of St. John may be put aside because the New Jerusalem is a dream, but whatever cause Spinoza and Bruno found for rejoicing lay in the common world of nature and mind. Spinoza talks about a " love for an object eternal and infinite " which "feeds the mind with joy alone." The same facts were before him which are before us, and we may assume that he did not shut his eyes to any of them. The indifference, therefore, and the despair of these latter days can hardly be due to the facts, but must be assigned to other causes ; and it would be a very interesting experiment to try what effect the presentation of every conclusion of modern thought would now have upon minds educated in healthy surroundings, and how far their joy in life would be affected thereby. We should probably discover that much of what we take to be the natural effect of purely legitimate deduction is simply disease, a something with which we are not to argue, but a something to be cured.

Pure speculation, however, is not in itself the goal, but the goal is nevertheless to be reached by thinking. It is declared to be a knowledge of the union between the mind and the whole of Nature, by which is not meant submission to Nature's ordinances, but *science*, which *is* that union. My aim, however, is not to be science for myself separately. It becomes felicity only when other people share it with me.

The reformation of intellectual procedure is therefore the first thing to be taken in hand, and it is startling to find ourselves face to face with the *summum bonum* on one page, and on the next with a discussion of the various methods by which we arrive at knowledge, so purely intelligent is our heavenward path to be !

The modes by which we arrive at knowledge are declared to be four : (1) by hearing, that is to say, by hearsay, tradition, or on authority ; (2) by loose experience ;[1] (3) by inference of a cause from an effect, or by deduction of a property from a universal ; and (4) by perception through essence, or knowledge of the proximate cause. In the *Ethic*

[1] *Vaga experientia* is a phrase of Bacon's—"Vaga enim experientia et se tantum sequens (ut superius dictum est) mera palpatio est, et homines potius stupefacit quam informat" (*Nov. Org.*, Aph. 100). It is as well to bear in mind this Baconian note for the sake of what will follow a little later when we have to consider the "eternal things."—TRANSLATOR.

(Schol. 2, Prop. 40, pt. 2) these four modes are arranged somewhat differently. The definition of · the fourth mode is there given as the knowledge which " advances from an adequate idea of the formal essence of certain attributes of God to the adequate knowledge of the essence of things."

Very few things, it is to be noticed, are discoverable by this fourth mode. What we call induction clearly comes under the third head, but the *Treatise* has very little to say about it, as the part in which Spinoza proposed to treat of empirical philosophy is missing. What he has to say about the third and fourth modes is characteristic. An example of the inference of a cause from an effect is the conclusion from sensation that the soul is united with the body, which union is the *cause* of sensation. Spinoza observes that the conclusion in such a case tells us nothing of the nature of the cause, and furthermore that we are liable, in making inferences of this kind, to conceive the cause too abstractly, and to imagine as separate entities what in effect is one. The example of deduction of a property from a universal is taken from optics. When we know the laws of vision we infer that the sun is larger than the earth. Here "something which is clearly perceived is attributed to the cause through the effect "—that is to say, something of the cause is clearly perceived through the effect ; but we perceive "nothing except properties ; not the essence of the particular thing." In other words, it is an inference. The example of the sun is perhaps not so plain as that taken from Euclid which immediately follows. A proposition in Euclid demonstrates that, in geometrical proportion, the product of the extremes is equal to that of the means. Hence, three terms being given, we are provided with a rule by which to find the fourth. This is deduction from a universal, but it is not the perception of essence, and in many of Euclid's propositions, where a complicated demonstration is necessary, we are still further from such a perception. We do not *see*, in fact, that a triangle is such a figure that its three angles must be equal to two right angles. Euclid draws a certain line parallel to one of the sides of the triangle, and compels us to admit the equality.

The examples which Spinoza gives of the fourth mode show that he intended simple, certain intuition. If I know the essence of the soul, I understand it to be united to the body. Union with body is the very meaning of soul. If two lines are parallel to a third they are parallel to one another, and so it is possible to see the proportionality of 2, 4, 3, 6 without Euclid. When we read that "the fourth mode alone grasps the adequate essence of the thing without danger of error, and therefore is the one of which we are to avail ourselves above all others," we hesitate, but in the *Ethic* the third kind is also declared (Prop. 41, pt. 2) to provide knowledge, which is necessarily true.

Having determined which is the best mode of acquiring knowledge, Spinoza proceeds to consider the way by which things are to be known by this method, but he first deals with the problem of certainty—How do I know that I know, how am I sure that the method itself rests upon the rock, and that all science is not a delusion ? He points out the absurdity of the infinite regress. If it be necessary that I should know that I know, it is necessary that I should know that I know that I know.

The sophistry of the infinite regress might be applied to prove that no tool which men use could ever have been invented ; for to make it, another tool must have been forged by the hammer, and to forge the hammer, another hammer must have been needed. The intellect has, by its own native force, certain intellectual instruments, by the use of which it acquires other instruments and so becomes wise. What is true of the workman's tools is true of the tools of the mind, or of *ideas,* taking the word *idea* in the second of the senses which has been given to it (p. x). I have an idea or thought or concept of Peter. This idea is something objectively real, but is not Peter. It may therefore be the object of another idea, and so on. Now it is perfectly clear that the knowledge of Peter must be the idea of Peter. It cannot be a condition of that knowledge that there should be an idea of the idea ; nay, rather, the idea of Peter is a condition of the idea of the idea. *The objective essence is certitude,* and there is nothing more to be said. In the scholium to the 43rd proposition of the second book of the *Ethic* Spinoza explains himself more fully : "No one who has a true idea is ignorant that a true idea

involves the highest certitude ; to have a true idea
signifying just this—to know a thing perfectly or
as well as possible. No one, in fact, can doubt this,
unless he supposes an idea to be something dumb,
like a picture on a tablet, instead of being a mode
of thought, that is to say, intelligence itself. Moreover, I ask, who can know that he understands a
thing unless he first of all understands that thing ?
—that is to say, who can know that he is certain
of anything unless he is first of all certain of that
thing ? Then, again, what can be clearer or more
certain than a true idea as the standard of truth ?
Just as light reveals both itself and the darkness, so
truth is the criterion of itself and of the false. . . .
With regard to the last-mentioned point—how a
man can know that he has an idea which agrees
with that of which it is the idea—I have shown
almost more times than enough that he knows it
simply because he has an idea which agrees with
that of which it is the idea—that is to say, because
truth is its own standard. We must remember,
besides, that our mind, in so far as it truly perceives
things, is a part of the infinite intellect of God
(Coroll., Prop. 11, pt. 2), and therefore it must
be that the clear and distinct ideas of the mind are
as true as those of God."

Is every man, then, who, to use Spinoza's
language, "has an idea of Peter," justified in his
confidence that he has a true idea ? Spinoza does
not say that. What he does say is that there is
no external justification of confidence, that any
attempt to find an external justification is suicidal,

and that the true idea carries certitude with, it.
We find him afterwards adding perfect clearness
and also capacity for development to the criteria
of certainty—that is to say, the true idea is in-
wardly consistent. From the last sentence, quoted
from the *Ethic*, we see how impossible it was for
Spinoza to doubt the validity of the true or
adequate idea. The true or adequate idea is not
a mere chance *representation* varying with the
light or with the obliquity or surface of the mirror :
it is *the* thought of the thing, the thing itself considered as thought, or, as Spinoza calls it, God's
thought.

It may be observed here that Spinoza's problem
is a little larger than that of certainty as debated,
say, between Mill and Spencer, although the latter
is included in the former. Spinoza's argument is
a reply not only to those who require a test of the
truth of a geometrical axiom, but also to those who
doubt the validity of intellectual processes, and that
we possess any *knowledge* either of the world of
mind or matter.

We now come to a closer view of the method.
It is the search in due order for objective essences
or true ideas, and compelling the mind to carry
on its operations by the standard or rule thus
obtained, or, in other words to form ideas after the
pattern of the true idea.

Spinoza enumerates four classes of ideas—the
true idea ; the idea of the fancy (*idea ficta*),
which we might perhaps pretty accurately describe as *idea picta ;* the false idea, and the

doubtful idea. He begins with the *idea ficta.*
There can be no such idea of that which is
necessary or impossible, but only of that which
is possible ; and the less I know the more easily
I can fancy. The less I know of nature the
more easily I can fancy trees speaking, or ghosts,
or that nothing becomes something. God, who
knows everything, can fancy nothing. The test
which will discover the idea of the fancy is
clear and distinct apprehension of the subject and
predicate. Given a clear idea of a tree and of
speech, it is impossible to join tree and speech
together. It follows, therefore, that the idea of
a perfectly simple object is clear and distinct ; that
in the case of a complex idea, confusion will cease
if we divide it into simple parts and attend to each
separately ; and that the idea of the fancy is
begotten by putting together different confusing
ideas and "attending" to them without admitting
their reality.

The false idea differs from the idea of the imagination merely in the assent which the former involves,
and the cure of the latter is that of the former.
Under this head Spinoza returns to what he has
said before about the impossibility of an external
test of truth. An architectural design is not false,
although no such design ever existed, or ever will
exist ; and, on the other hand, if I say what I do
not know to be true, it is false, even if it should
happen to be true. Therefore, says Spinoza, "the
form of true thought . . . must depend upon the
power itself and nature of the intellect." He gives

another example, to make himself clearer. We
conceive a globe to be formed by the revolution of
a semi-circle. Although no globe may actually
have been produced in that way, the concept is
true. Mark, however, that the bare affirmation of
the revolution of a semicircle, unless we affirm it
for the sake of defining the globe, would be false.
The simple idea of the semicircle, or of motion, or of
rest, is true, but the idea of the moving semicircle
is false, unless under the condition that we use it in
order to describe the globe. Falsity, then, is affirmation beyond the concept. Parenthetically we
have the remark that a fruitful cause of deception
is the presentation of certain things both by the
imagination and the intellect. For example, the
Stoics had before them soul, immortality, body, and
a theorem that the most subtle bodies penetrated
others. The theorem they understood, but soul
and body, although they can be conceived by the
intellect, were imagined confusedly, and hence it
was asserted that the soul was most subtle and penetrated the body.

Spinoza takes occasion to warn us against deductions from abstract axioms and universals. So much
is clearly his intention, but the passage (p. 42) is
difficult because of its peculiar phraseology. We
have "primary elements of Nature," "fountain and
origin of Nature," "origin of Nature," all used for
the same thing. We are told that it is not an
abstract nor universal, nor yet has any similitude
with mutable things. "No confusion with regard
to its idea is to be feared, provided only we possess

the standard of truth which we have just set forth.
For this is Being, one, infinite ; that is to say, it is
all Being, and beside it there is no other Being."
Let us see if we can obtain any clue from the consideration of parallel passages. " The good method
(p. 19) shows in what manner the mind is to be
guided according to the standard of an existing true
idea. But, since the relation which exists between
two ideas is the same as the relation between the
formal essences of those ideas, it follows that the
knowledge which arises from reflection on the idea
of the most perfect Being will be more excellent
than the knowledge arising from reflection on other
ideas ; that is to say, that will be the most perfect
method which shows in what manner the mind is
to be directed in accordance with the standard of
the given idea of the most perfect Being." Again
(p. 20), " It is clear that in order that our mind
may exactly reproduce the pattern of Nature, it
must draw all its ideas from that idea which reproduces the origin and fountain of the whole of
Nature, so that it may also become the source of
other ideas." Once more (p. 21), we are told
that "the good method is that which shows
in what manner the mind is to be directed in
accordance with the standard of a given true idea,"
and " in the investigation of Nature " we shall suc-
ceed if we " acquire ideas in their proper order,
according to the standard of a given true idea." It
is our duty "to make systematic investigation in
accordance with the standard of some existing true
idea " (p. 24), and hence the first part of the

method (p. 24) "is to distinguish a true idea from all other perceptions," and the second part consists in the rules "whereby unknown things may be perceived in accordance with this standard."

By the "standard of a true idea" are meant the marks of a true idea—simplicity, clearness, &c.— and the mind is "directed in accordance with the standard of a given true idea" when it takes the true idea as a model and proceeds by the third and fourth modes of acquiring knowledge (p. 12) ; the third mode, it should particularly be borne in mind, including induction as well as deduction. The "primary elements," "fountain and origin," are not abstracts nor universals, nor have "*any similitude with mutable things*," but are the "fixed and eternal things" of which we shall hear later on. The whole process, then, up to the introduction of the Being, one and infinite, consists in the acquisition of ideas which shall have the marks of the true idea, perfect clearness for example ; the application of the third and fourth modes of knowledge, and the use of the "fixed and eternal things." But what is this Being which is one and infinite and a standard of truth ? He is undoubtedly the God of the *Ethic*, and God becomes the supreme standard in the sense that the better we know Him *as Spinoza understood Him* the more complete or accurate is the "standard of the true idea." In this connection the twenty-eighth proposition of the fourth book of the *Ethic* may be quoted. "To understand, therefore, is the absolute virtue of the mind. But the highest thing which the mind can understand

is God (as we have already demonstrated), and
therefore the highest virtue of the mind is to
understand or know God." It is surprising in a
psychological treatise to find the Being one and
infinite, besides whom there is no other Being,
introduced as a test of truth ; but Spinoza perpetu-
ally surprises us by his use—or shall we say by his
realisation—of theological terms.

The discussion of the " doubtful idea," excepting
the criticism of Descartes, which is explained in the
note on p. 45, needs no remark, and Spinoza con-
cludes what he had to say about the first part of
the method with a few words on memory and forgetfulness, and by some important observations on
the imagination and the power of words. It is the
imagined idea or image which is the source of error.
Spinoza does not care how we define the imagination, if we do not confound it with the intellect,
or its laws with intellectual laws, and if we consider it as something which reduces the mind to
passivity. Commonly it is thought that what we
can imagine we can understand, and that if we find
it easy to imagine, it is easy to understand. The
truth is, that the imagination, by the presentation
of a picture of what cannot be pictured, but ought
to be *thought*, continually prevents understanding.
Words afford many instances of the mischief wrought
by the imagination, inasmuch as positive ideas,
which the imagination cannot paint, are expressed
negatively, and hence it is concluded that they are
not positive, but mere negations. Such positives,
for example, are " infinite," " increate," " indepen-

dent," "immortal," "incorporeal." The distinction
between picture and thought is one on which
Spinoza earnestly insists, not only in the *Treatise*
but in the *Ethic*, and it may be said that it is
impossible to proceed a single step with him unless
this distinction be recognised.

We now come to the second part of the Method,
which (p. 24) consists in "laying down rules whereby unknown things may be perceived in accordance
with the standard of the true idea," or, as we have
just said, in accordance with the third and fourth
modes of knowledge, which include both induction
and deduction. Of induction, or the inference of
the cause from the effect (p. 9), Spinoza here says
nothing, but at once proceeds to define definition,
for the best conclusion will be drawn from " a true
and legitimate definition." A definition of this kind
must explain " the innermost essence of the thing,
and not assume in place of it certain properties."
An example of a false definition, which assumes
certain properties, is that of a circle as a figure such
that lines drawn from its centre to the circumference
are equal, and an example of true definition is that
of a circle as a figure described by any line of which
one extremity is fixed and the other movable. If a
thing be a created thing the definition must include
the proximate cause, for then only can we deduce
properties. The proximate cause of the circle is the
revolution of the fixed line. What is surprising in
Spinoza's statement in the first place is the declara-
tion that " the *whole* of the second part turns upon
the assignment of the conditions of a good defini-

tion and upon the mode of discovering good definitions," nothing being said about the inference of the
cause from the effect ; and secondly, the decisive
and, to us, most strange doctrine that a good definition is the best means by which to arrive at truth.
On the first point it is impossible, considering the
present fragmentary condition of the *Treatise*, to
say anything with certainty, but we cannot believe
that Spinoza intended to proceed by definition
alone ; in fact, he himself says he did not. With
regard to the second point, we must bear in mind
what Spinoza evidently intends by definition. He
means scientific description, just as CO_2 is a definition of carbon dioxide. There is no doubt, moreover, that amongst philosophers of that time it was
believed to be possible to imitate the success of
mathematics and to obtain definitions which would
be engines of discovery in what we call natural
philosophy, and to some extent there was ground
for their belief, for we really have acquired "definitions," as Spinoza understood them, which are fruitful in results. Then, again, Spinoza was probably
thinking, as he is always thinking, of ethic, where
definitions are of the utmost importance. They
are, as Mill says (*Logic*, v. 1, p. 170, ed. 1862),
the result of "inquiries not so much to determine
what is, as what should be, the meaning of a name."
Four conditions are enumerated as necessary for the
definition of a thing increate. On the first, third,
and fourth it is not necessary to say anything ; the
second, "given the definition of the thing, there
should be no possibility of questioning whether it

exists," raises the whole controversy whether, to use the very first words of the *Ethic*, it is possible to think an object " whose nature cannot be conceived unless existing," or whether, as Kant says, " we must always step outside our concept of an object in order to attribute to it existence." That is much too large a question to be debated here.

We are " to advance as strictly as possible, according to the series of causes, from one real entity to another real entity . . . " but by the series of causes and entities we are not to understand " the series of individual mutable things, but the series only of things fixed and eternal." These fixed and eternal things, although they are singulars, are omnipresent, and in this respect resemble universals, or are like the genera of definitions, and are the proximate causes of all things. Their laws are the codes according to which all individual things are produced and are ordered, and individual things depend on them so intimately and essentially that the former without the latter can neither be nor be conceived.

There has been much difference of opinion as to what Spinoza understands by these fixed and eternal things. They much resemble the Baconian Forms. The Forms are not material causes, and are few in number ; [1] they are the laws by which individual bodies act ; [2] they embrace the unity of nature in substances the most unlike ; [3] they are such that, given the Form, the nature infallibly follows, and if

---

[1] *Advancement of Learning*, bk. ii.
[2] *Nov. Org.*, bk. ii. 2-17.   [3] *Ibid.*, bk. ii. 3.

taken away, the nature infallibly vanishes : the true form also deduces the given nature from some source of being which is inherent in more natures, and which is better known in the natural order of things than the Form itself." [1] The Form is the very thing itself, the real as contrasted with the apparent, or the internal with the external, or the thing in reference to the universe with the thing in reference to man ; it exalts to new efficients and new modes of operation.[2] Finally, as an example, Motion, with certain qualifications, is declared to be the Form of Heat.[3]

Sir Frederick Pollock [4] thinks that by the fixed and eternal things are intended the things immediately produced by God, mentioned in the letter to Tschirnhausen of July 25, 1675—that is to say, "the infinite intellect" in thought and "motion and rest" in extension ; and what Spinoza means is that, so far as physical things are concerned, Nature is ultimately explicable by dynamical laws. Unfortunately the *Treatise* says nothing more on this subject, nor is it taken up again in the *Ethic*. My own opinion inclines rather to more or less identification with the Forms, and we know that Spinoza had studied Bacon profoundly, but in the face of Sir Frederick Pollock's criticism the matter must be left doubtful. One thing is clear, that they much resemble Spinoza's own "true and legitimate definitions." [5]

---

[1] *Ibid.*, bk. ii. 4. [2] *Ibid.*, bk. ii. 13.
[3] *Ibid.*, bk. ii. 20. [4] *Spinoza*, p. 152.
[5] There are, as Miss Stirling has pointed out to me, some remarkable points of correspondence between the "eternal

In order that we may arrive at the knowledge of eternal things and obtain definitions for them, we must first of all examine the properties of the intellect. Spinoza enumerates eight, and with some of them he has dealt previously, but there are one or two which are new and are particularly worth notice. The second and third, for example, are as follows : The intellect can form independent ideas, or ideas which are not derivative from any others. Quantity, for instance—not any particular quantity, but quantity simply as quantity—is an independent idea, but the idea of motion, as it cannot exist without that of quantity, is derivative. The independent ideas express infinity, but those which are derivative express limitation. The fifth property of the intellect is that it perceives things under a certain " form of eternity," but the imagination sees limited number, duration, and quantity. In the *Cogitata Metaphysica* eternity and indefinite

things" and the Platonic "ideas." For example, in the *Phædo* the idea of equality is the truth of equality ; it is that at which the equality of equal things aims ; ideas or essences are self-existent and unchanging, and are causes. In the *Republic* (bk. v.) the idea is the " object of real knowledge " ; the many (bk. vi.) are " seen but not known, and the ideas are known but not seen." Ideas are also in the same book compared with the figures which are the subject of inquiry by the geometer, who does not think of visible forms and reason about them. Ideas are archetypes in the mind of God (bk. x.), and the eternal pattern (*Timæus*) which He had before Him in the creation of the world. Without ideas there is nothing on which the mind can rest, and philosophy is impossible (*Parmenides*) ; they are the unity (*Sophist*) in which the many are comprehended ; they are (*Philebus*) incapable of generation or destruction, retain a permanent individuality, and though entire and divided from the world of generation may be conceived as dispersed and multiplied in it.—See also the summary of the Platonic doctrine of ideas in the index to Jowett's *Plato*, vol. v. p. 440, ed. 1892.

duration are carefully distinguished. To necessary truths *duration*, however prolonged, is inapplicable. "Nobody will ever say that the essence of a circle or a triangle, in so far as it is an eternal truth, has existed for a longer time at the present moment than at the time of Adam" (*Cog. Met.* pt. ii. chap. i.). In a letter to Meyer of April 20, 1663, Spinoza insists that eternity is a thing to be grasped not by the imagination but by the intellect alone, and that "through duration we can explain only the existence of modes ; but through eternity that of substance—that is to say, an infinite enjoyment of existence, or rather (although the Latin does not lend itself to such a mode of expression) of Being (*essendi*)." The second corollary to the forty-fourth proposition of the second book of the *Ethic* declares that "it is of the nature of reason to perceive things under a certain form of eternity," the proof being that reason discovers things to be *necessary*, and necessity is the eternal nature of God. In the scholium to the twenty-ninth proposition of the fifth book we are told that, "Things are conceived by us as actual in two ways : either in so far as we conceive them to exist with relation to a fixed time and place, or in so far as we conceive them to be contained in God, and to follow from the necessity of the Divine nature. But those things which are conceived in this second way as true or real we conceive under the form of eternity, and their ideas involve the eternal and infinite essence of God." Once more, according to the thirteenth proposition of the same book, "eternity is the very essence of God, in so far as that essence involves necessary existence." Eternal truths are therefore necessary truths, truths to which time is inapplicable. There cannot have been a time when the three angles of a triangle became equal to two right angles, and everything seen by the reason is seen under this "form."

Here the *Treatise* breaks off abruptly—*Reliqua desiderantur*, say the editors.

The object of this preface has not been to examine fully all the points raised by Spinoza, for such an examination would involve a History of Philosophy and a Critique of the Reason. All that has been attempted has been an analysis, with a commentary here and there, in order to explain some difficulties. That there are many unexplained is but too true, but those who will take the trouble to read the *Treatise* carefully will probably admit that, although it may often be easy to offer something to stand in place of a solution, to give *the* solution is not easy. It is better in such cases to remain silent or confess ignorance than to impose a meaning which was not intended. Nevertheless, to repeat the words of the *Advice to the Reader*, although there are so many defects in the book, "it contains much that is remarkable and useful and not a little profitable to the sincere inquirer after truth," and that it is suggestive to a singular degree nobody who will take any pains with it will, I think, doubt. It is necessary to add that, although care has been taken to make Spinoza's meaning as intelligible as possible, it has not been thought right to sacrifice literal accuracy to style, and consequently, the ruggednesses noticed in the *Advice* reappear in the translation.

A TREATISE CONCERNING THE EMENDATION OF THE INTELLECT AND OF THE WAY IN WHICH IT IS BEST LED TO THE TRUE KNOWLEDGE OF THINGS.

(The Preliminary Advice to the Reader has been already given in the Preface.—TRANS.)

AFTER experience had taught me that all things which are ordinarily encountered in common life are vain and futile, and when I saw that all things which occasioned me any anxiety or fear had in themselves nothing of good or evil, except in so far as the mind was moved by them; I at length determined to inquire if there were anything which was a true good capable of imparting itself, by which the mind could be solely affected to the exclusion of all else ; whether, indeed, anything existed by whose discovery and acquisition I might be put in possession of a joy continuous and supreme to all eternity. I say that *I at length determined;* for at the first glance it appeared to me to be foolish to be willing to part with something certain for something then uncertain. I saw, forsooth, the advantages which accrue from honour and riches, and that I should be forced to abstain from seeking these if I wished to apply myself seriously to another and new undertaking ; and if, by chance, perfect happiness should lie in those things, I perceived that I must go without it ; but if, on the other hand, it did not lie in them, and I applied myself only to them, I must then also go without the highest happiness. I turned it over, therefore, in my mind whether it might not perchance be possible to carry out my new purpose or, at least, to arrive at some certainty with regard to it, without changing the order and ordinary plan of my life, a thing I had often attempted in vain. Now, the things which generally present themselves in life, and are considered by men as the highest good, so far as can be gathered from their actions, are included in these three, riches, honour, and sensual indulgence. By these three the mind is so distracted, that it is scarcely possible for it to think of any other good thing. For example, as regards sensual indulgence, the mind is engrossed by it to such a degree as to rest in it as in some good, and is thereby entirely prevented from thinking of anything else, but, after it has been satisfied, there follows a very great melancholy, which, if it does not check the action of the mind, nevertheless disturbs and blunts it. Through the pursuit of honours and riches also the mind is not a little distracted, especially [1] if the

---

[1] This might be explained at greater length and more distinctly, that is to say, by distinguishing riches which are sought either for their own sake, or for the sake of honour, or for the

latter are sought for their own sake, because in that case they are supposed to be the highest good. By honour the mind is even more distracted ; for it is always regarded as a good in itself, and, as it were, the ultimate end to which everything is directed. Again, in the case of honour and riches there is no repentance, as in the case of sensual indulgence, but the more we have of them, the more our joy is increased ; and consequently we are more and more incited to increase them : nevertheless, if by any chance our expectations are deceived, then very great sorrow arises. Finally, honour is a great hindrance to us, because it is necessary, if we would attain it, to direct our lives according to the notions of men—that is to say, by avoiding what they commonly avoid, and seeking what they commonly seek.

Since, therefore, I saw that all these things stood in the way of my devoting myself to any new purpose ; that, in fact, they were so opposed to it, that either they or it must be relinquished, I was compelled to inquire what was most useful to me, for as I have said, it seemed as if I were willing to lose a certain good for that which was uncertain. But after I had reflected a little on the subject, I discovered, in the first place, that if forsaking riches and honour and sensual indulgence, I should address myself to my new purpose, I should be giving up a good uncertain in its very nature, as may clearly be

sake of sensual desire, or for the sake of health and the promotion of science and art, but this is reserved for the proper place, for the present is not a suitable opportunity for investigating this subject more closely (*Sp.*).

seen from what has already been said, for one uncertain not in its very nature (for I sought a good
which was stable), but only so far as its attainment
was concerned, and after careful reflection, I came
to see that, if only I could apply myself wholly to
thought, I should then be giving up certain evils
for a certain good. For I saw that I was situated
in the greatest danger, and I forced myself to seek
with all my strength a remedy, even although it
might be uncertain, just as a sick man suffering
from a mortal disease, who foresees certain death
unless a remedy be applied, is forced to seek it with
all his strength, even though it be uncertain, for
therein lies the whole of his hope. All those things,
however, which the majority of persons pursue, not
only contribute no means whereby to preserve our
being, but even are a hindrance to its preservation.
They frequently cause the destruction of those who
possess them,[1] and always cause the destruction of
those who are possessed by them.

For there are very many examples of men who
have suffered persecution even to death for the sake
of their riches, and also of men, who, in order that
they might obtain wealth, have exposed themselves
to so many dangers that at length they have paid
with their lives the penalty of their folly. Nor are
there fewer examples of men, who, in order that
they might obtain honour, or guard it, have endured
most miserable calamities ; and, lastly, innumerable
are the examples of those who, through excess of

---

[1] This will be more accurately demonstrated (*Sp.*). Not in the
Treatise as we now have it.—TRANS.

sensual indulgence, have hastened their death. The cause of these evils appeared to be that all happiness or unhappiness solely depends upon the quality of the object to which we are attached by love. For on account of that which is not loved no strife will arise, there will be no sorrow if it perishes, no jealousy if it is appropriated by another, no fear, no hatred, and, in a word, no agitations of the mind. All these, however, arise from the love of that which is perishable, as all those things are of which we have just spoken. But love for an object eternal and infinite feeds the mind with joy alone, and a joy which is free from all sorrow. This is something greatly to be desired and to be sought with all our strength.

But not without reason did I use the words *if I could but apply myself wholly to thought.* For although I saw all this so clearly in my mind, I could not therefore put aside all avarice, sensual desire, and love of honour. This one thing I saw, that so long as my mind was occupied with these thoughts, so long it was turned away from the things mentioned above, and seriously reflected on the new purpose. This comforted me greatly. For I saw that those evils were not of such a kind that they would not yield to remedies. And although in the beginning these intervals were rare and lasted but for a very short time, nevertheless, when the true good was by degrees better known to me, they became more frequent and longer, especially when I came to see that the acquisition of wealth, or sensual desire and love of honour, are injurious so long as they are sought for their own sake and not as means for other things ; but if they are sought as means they will be enjoyed in moderation and will not be injurious : on the contrary, they will be very conducive to the end for which they are sought, as we shall show in the proper place.

Here I will explain, but only briefly, what I understand by a true good, and at the same time what is the highest good. In order that this may be rightly understood, it is to be observed that the words " good " and " evil " are only used relatively, so that one and the same thing may be called good and evil according to its different relations, just as from different points of view it may be called perfect or imperfect. For nothing considered in its own nature can be called perfect or imperfect, especially after we have discerned that everything comes to pass according to an eternal order and according to fixed laws of Nature. But since human weakness cannot reach that order by its own thought, and meanwhile man can imagine a human nature much stronger than his own, and sees no obstacle to prevent his acquiring such a nature, he is urged to seek the means which may lead him to such perfection. Everything, therefore, which may be a means by which to arrive thereat, he calls a true good, but the highest good is to obtain, with as many other individuals as possible, the enjoyment of that nature.[1]

[1] " Perfection, therefore, and imperfection are really only modes of thought, that is to say, notions which we are in the habit of forming from the comparison with one another of individuals of the same species or genus."—*Ethic*, pt. iv. Preface.—TRANS.

But what that nature is we shall show in the proper place—that it is a knowledge of the union between the mind and the whole of Nature.[1] This, therefore, is the end towards which I strive—to acquire this nature and to endeavour that others may acquire it with me—that is to say, it is essential to my happiness to try to make many others understand what I understand, so that their intellect and desire may entirely agree with my intellect and desire. In order to achieve this end, it is necessary[2] to understand so much of Nature as may be sufficient for acquiring the desired nature ; then to form a society such as is desirable for enabling as many people as possible with the greatest ease and security to acquire it. Furthermore, we must pay attention to Moral Philosophy as well as to the science of the education of children, and because health is by no means an insignificant means to the attainment of this end, the whole of medicine is to be studied. Because also many things which are difficult are rendered easier by art and we can thereby gain much time and comfort in life, Mechanics are by no means to be despised. But above everything a means of healing the mind must be sought out, and of purifying it as much as possible at the outset so that it may happily understand things without error and as completely as possible. Hence

---

[1] These things are explained more fully in their proper place (*Sp.*). Not in the Treatise as we now have it, but see p. 13. —TRANS.

[2] Observe that I here only desire to enumerate the sciences necessary to our purpose, and not to trouble myself with their sequence (*Sp.*).

everybody can now see that I wish to direct all the sciences to a single end and purpose,[1] namely, that we may reach that highest human perfection of which we have spoken. Therefore everything in the sciences which in no way advances us towards our end will be rejected as useless, that is to say, in one word, all our actions as well as our thoughts are to be directed to this end. Since, however, while we are seeking to attain it and are endeavouring to constrain our intellect into the right way, it is necessary to live, we must first of all assume certain rules of life to be good. They are these :—

I. To speak and act in accordance with the notions of the majority, provided no hindrance thereby arises to the attainment of our purpose. For we can obtain not a little profit from them, if we conform as much as possible to their notions, and, besides, in this way they will lend friendly ears to listen to the truth.

II. To indulge in pleasures only so far as is consistent with the preservation of health.

III. To seek only so much of wealth or of anything else as is sufficient to preserve life and health, and to conform to such customs of the State as are not opposed to our purpose.[2]

----

[1] There is a single end for all the sciences, to which they all must be directed (*Sp.*).

[2] Descartes also had his provisory code and the difference between the two is noteworthy. Descartes' first rule was to obey the laws and customs of his country and abide firmly by its Faith. Secondly, to be firm and resolute in his actions, and when once he had adopted an opinion to adhere to it. Thirdly,

Having laid down these rules, I will attempt·that which stands first, and is to be achieved before any-thing, that is to say, to improve the intellect and make it fit to understand things in the way which is necessary in order to obtain our end. To do this, natural order requires that I should here review all the kinds of knowledge which I have hitherto pos-sessed whereby to affirm or deny positively, in order that I may choose the best of them all, and at the same time may begin to know my powers and that nature which I wish to perfect.

If I consider accurately, they may all be reduced generally to four.

I. There is the knowledge which we derive from hearing [1] or from some arbitrary sign.

II. There is the knowledge which we derive from vague experience, that is to say, from experience which is independent of the intellect and which is so called only because it presents itself casually and we have no experimental proof to the contrary. There-fore it abides with us undisturbed.

III. There is the knowledge which arises when the essence of a thing is deduced from another thing, but not adequately. This happens [2] when we either

to attempt to conquer himself, rather than circumstances (*Dis-course on Method*, pt. iii.).

[1] *Ex auditu*, from hearing, hearsay, or simply on authority.—TRANS.

[2] When this is the case, we understand nothing of the cause through that which we contemplate in the effect. This is clear from the fact that the cause is then explained only in general terms, as, for example, *therefore there is something; therefore there is some power*, &c. It is also clear from the negative ex-pression *therefore this or that is not*, &c. In the second case,

infer the cause from some effect, or when we make an inference from some universal which is always accompanied by some property.

IV. Finally there is the knowledge which arises when a thing is perceived through its essence alone, or through the knowledge of its proximate cause.

All this I will illustrate by examples. From mere *hearing* I know my birthday, and that I had certain parents, and other things of the same kind which I have never doubted. Through *vague experience* I know that I shall die, for I affirm it because I have seen other people die of the same nature as myself, although they have not all lived equally long, nor have they died of the same disease. Again through vague experience I also know that oil is the proper food for feeding flame, and that water is fit for extinguishing it ; I know also that a dog is a barking animal and man is a rational animal, and in this way I have learned nearly everything which appertains to the service of life. We deduce *from some other thing* in this way : when we clearly perceive that we are sensible of a particular body and no other, then we clearly deduce, I say, from that perception that our mind[1] is united to that body, and that

something which is clearly conceived is attributed to the cause through the effect, as we shall show in the example ; but nothing except properties ; not the essence of the particular thing (*Sp.*).

[1] From this example is plainly to be seen what I have just noted ;[2] for by that union we understand nothing except the sensation itself, which is an effect, from which we conclude a cause of which we understand nothing (*Sp.*).

[2] Under III., where it is pointed out that the deduction is not adequate. The Latin is "præter sensationem ipsam, *effectus*

this union is the cause of that sensation,[1] but we cannot understand directly from it the nature of that union and of sensation. Again, after I have come to know the nature of sight, and at the same time that it has this property, that at a great distance we see one and the same thing to be less than when we see it near at hand, I deduce that the sun is greater than he appears to be, and other conclusions of the same kind.

Finally, a thing is perceived through *its essence alone*, when from the fact that I have known something, I understand what it is to have known something ;[2] as, for instance, from the fact that I have known the essence of the soul I understand it to be united to the body. By this kind of knowledge we know that two and three are five, and that if there be two lines parallel to a third, they are parallel to one another. But the things which I can as yet understand by this kind of knowledge are very few.

scilicet, ex quo," &c. There is probably a mistake here, and Saisset's emendation of *effectum* is most likely correct.—TRANS.

[1] Such a conclusion, although it may be certain, is nevertheless not sufficiently safe, unless great precautions are taken. For unless we take great care we immediately fall into errors, inasmuch as when we conceive things thus abstractly, and not through their true essence, they are at once confounded by the imagination. For that which in itself is one we imagine to be multifold, and to those things which we conceive abstractly, separately, and confusedly, we apply names which are used to distinguish familiar objects. Hence it comes to pass that the former are imagined in the same way in which we are accustomed to imagine the things to which the names were first applied (*Sp.*).

[2] The expression in this paragraph is obscure. The phrase " I understand what it is to have known something " (scio quid hoc sit aliquid nosse) is equivalent to " I comprehend the whole knowledge of the thing : I comprehend the whole act of knowing and the thing known."—TRANS.

In order that all these things may be better understood I will give only one example as follows.
Three numbers are given : a fourth is required
which shall be to the third as the second is to the
first. In such a case merchants generally say that
they know what is to be done in order to find the
fourth, because they have not as yet forgotten the
rule which they heard nakedly, without any demonstration, from their teachers. Others from their
experience of particular cases construct a universal
axiom. When, for example, the fourth number is
self-evident, as in the series 2, 4, 3, 6, they see that
if the second be multiplied by the third and the product divided by the first the quotient is 6. Since
they observe that the quotient is the same number
which, without this rule, they knew to be the proportional, they conclude that the rule is always
valid for the discovery of a fourth proportional
number. Mathematicians, however, by the help of
the demonstration of Euclid, Prop. 19, bk. vii.,
know what numbers are proportional to one another—
that is to say, that from the nature and property of
proportion a number which is the product of the
first and fourth is equal to a number which is the
product of the second and third, but they do not see
the adequate proportionality of the given numbers,
or if they do see it, it is not by the help of this proposition, but intuitively and without any calculation.

In order to select the best of these kinds of
knowledge it is necessary that we should briefly
enumerate what are the necessary means to the
attainment of our end. They are these :—

1. To know exactly our own nature which we desire to perfect, and at the same time so much of the nature of things as is necessary.

2. To form correct inductions with regard to the differences, agreements, and oppositions of things.

3. To understand properly how far they can and how far they cannot be acted upon.[1]

4. To compare the result with the nature and power of man. It will then clearly appear what is the highest perfection to which man can attain. Having thus considered these matters, let us see what kind of knowledge we ought to choose.

As to the first, without taking into account that it is something altogether uncertain, it is self-evident that from hearing, as appears from our example, no essence of a thing can be perceived, and since, as will afterwards be seen, the particular existence of a thing is not known unless its essence be known, we clearly infer that all the certainty which we derive from hearing must be distinguished from science. For no one can be affected by simple hearing unless his own intellect has first acted.[2]

As to the second, no one can say that he obtains thereby the idea of that proportion which he seeks.

[1] *Quid possint pati, quid non*—what they can and cannot be *made to do*. These four paragraphs contain in a measure the exposition of the union with Nature (see p. 7). A knowledge of that union was declared to be the end towards which we strive and the highest good. Spinoza, before going any further, desires us clearly to keep in view our object, to know what we can do and what Nature can be made to do, so that the perfection may be reached.—TRANS.

[2] Here I intend at some time or other to treat more fully of experience, and I shall examine more fully the mode of procedure of the empirical and recent philosophers (*Sp.*).

Not only is it something altogether uncertain, not only is no definite object in view, but by means of it nothing of natural objects is ever perceived save accidents, which are never clearly understood unless the essences of the things be previously known. Therefore also this method is to be set aside.

By the third it may in some measure be said that we have an idea of the thing, and that thence we can conclude without danger of error, but, nevertheless, this by itself will not be the means whereby we may obtain our perfection.

The fourth mode alone grasps the adequate essence of the thing without danger of error, and therefore is the one of which we are to avail ourselves above all others. We will take care to explain in what manner it is to be applied, so that by this kind of knowledge unknown things may be understood by us, and how this may be achieved as succinctly as possible.[1]

After we have discovered what kind of knowledge is necessary for us, the way and method are to be exhibited by which the things which are to be known may be known by this kind of knowledge. To this end, we must first consider that there is here no search *ad infinitum ;* that is to say, in order that the best method of discovering the truth may be found, there is no need of another method

[1] The four modes of knowledge are arranged somewhat differently in the *Ethic.* (See Schol. 2, Prop. 40, pt. ii.) The definition of the fourth mode as there given is that which "advances from an adequate idea of the formal essence of certain attributes of God to the adequate knowledge of the essence of things."—TRANS.

for investigating the method of investigating · the truth, and in order that the second method may be investigated there is no need of a third and so on *ad infinitum ;* for in this way we shall never arrive at a knowledge of the truth, nor indeed at any knowledge. It is the same with tools ; and the argument proceeds in the same way. For example, in order that iron may be forged, we need a hammer ; and if we are to have a hammer, we must make one. To this end we need another hammer and other instruments ; and to obtain these we shall need other instruments and so on *ad infinitum.* Thus anybody might fruitlessly endeavour to prove that men are unable to forge iron. But inasmuch as men at the beginning, with instruments furnished by nature, were able to make certain very easy things, although with great labour and imperfectly, and with these, when they were finished, made other and more difficult things with less labour and more perfectly, and thus by degrees, advancing from the most simple productions to tools, and from tools to other productions and tools, were able to accomplish with small labour so many and such difficult things, so also the intellect,[1] by its own native force, forms for itself intellectual instruments by which it acquires additional strength for other intellectual works,[2] and from these works, other instruments or power of further discovery, and thus by degrees

---

[1] By native force I understand that in us which is not caused by external causes, as will be hereafter explained in my Philosophy (*Sp.*).

[2] Here they are called works (*opera*). What they are will be explained in my Philosophy (*Sp.*).

advances until it reaches the pinnacle of wisdom. That this is the way in which the intellect proceeds will be easily seen, provided only we understand what is the method of investigating the truth, and what are those instruments furnished by nature which alone are required for the production of other instruments from them in order to advance further. To show this I proceed as follows :—

[1] A true idea (for we have a true idea), is something different from its object ; for a circle is one thing, and the idea of a circle something different. For the idea of a circle is not something which, like a circle, has a circumference and a centre, nor is the idea of a body the body itself. Since therefore the idea is something different from its object, it will be something intelligible *per se*, that is to say, the idea, so far as regards its formal essence, can be the object of some other objective essence, and again this other objective essence, considered in itself, will also be something real and intelligible, and so on indefinitely. Peter, for example, is something real, but the true idea of Peter is the objective essence of Peter, and something real in itself and altogether different from Peter. Since, therefore, the idea of Peter is something real, having its own proper essence, it will also be something intelligible, that is to say, the object of another idea, which will have in itself objectively everything which the idea of Peter has formally ; and,

---

[1] Observe that here we shall not only endeavour to make plain what has just been said, but also that our mode of procedure up to this point has been correct, together with other matters very necessary to be known (*Sp.*).

further, the idea of the idea of Peter has again its own essence, which also can be the object of another idea, and so on indefinitely. This anybody may discover for himself when he sees that he knows what Peter is, and also that he knows that he knows, and again knows that he knows that he knows, &c. Hence it is evident that, in order to understand the essence of Peter, it is not necessary to understand the idea itself of Peter, and much less the idea of the idea of Peter ; in other words, in order to know, it is not necessary for me to know that I know, and much less is it necessary to know that I know that I know—no more than in order to understand the essence of a triangle it is necessary to understand the essence of a circle.[1] Exactly the contrary is true of these ideas, for in order to know that I know, I must necessarily first of all know. Hence it is clear that certainty is nothing but the objective essence itself, that is to say, the mode in which we perceive formal essence is itself certainty. It is also clear that there is need of no other mark of the certainty of a truth than the possession of a true idea ; for as we have shown, in order to know, it is not

[1] Observe that we here make no inquiry as to the manner in which the first objective essence arises in us. That belongs to the investigation of nature, where these matters are more fully explained, and at the same time it is shown that beyond the idea there is no affirmation, negation, nor will (*Sp.*).

This latter thesis is the subject of the celebrated Prop. xlix. of the *Ethic*, pt. ii., with the accompanying Corollary and Scholium. Spinoza's doctrine is that there is no possibility of any exercise of the will beyond the intellect, or, in other words, that the will can only follow what the intellect discerns.— TRANS.

necessary for me to know that I know. Once
more, it is clear from what has been said that no
one can know what is perfect certainty unless he
possesses the adequate idea or objective essence
of any given thing, for certitude and objective
essence are one.

Since, therefore, truth needs no mark, but in
order to get rid of all doubt it is enough to have
the objective essences of things, or, what is the
same thing, ideas, it follows that the true method
is not to seek for a mark of truth after the acquisition of ideas, but that the true method is the way
through which truth itself, or the objective essences
of things, or ideas (for all these mean the same
thing), may be sought in due order.[1] Again, the
method must necessarily discuss reasoning, or the
process of understanding — that is to say, the
method is not a chain of reasoning for reaching
the understanding of the causes of things, still less
is it the actual understanding (τὸ *intelligere*) of the
causes of things, but it is the understanding what
a true idea is by distinguishing it from other perceptions, and by investigating its nature, thus
enabling us to learn our power of understanding,
and so to control our mind that it may understand
in accordance with that standard whatever is to be
understood, and also laying down certain rules to
help us and to prevent our mind from being
wearied by what is useless.

Hence we gather that the method is knowledge

---

[1] What to search in the mind means is explained in my
Philosophy (*Sp.*).

arising from reflection (*cognitio reflexiva*), or the idea of an idea ; and since there can be no idea of an idea unless there first exist an idea, therefore unless an idea first exist, there will be no method. That, therefore, will be the good method which shows in what manner the mind is to be guided according to the standard of an existing true idea.

But since the relation which exists between two ideas is the same as the relation between the formal essences of those ideas, it follows that the knowledge which arises from reflection on the idea of the most perfect Being will be more excellent than the knowledge arising from reflection on other ideas ; that is to say, that will be the most perfect method which shows in what manner the mind is to be directed in accordance with the standard of the given idea of the most perfect Being.

It is now easy to understand in what manner the mind, by understanding many things, at the same time acquires other instruments by means of which it may more easily advance in knowledge. For, as we may gather from what has already been said, there must before everything else exist in us a true idea which is as it were an innate instrument ; and when it is understood, the difference is at the same time understood which there is between such a perception and all others. Herein consists one part of method. And since it is self-evident that the more things the mind understands about Nature the better it understands itself, it is evident that this part of Method will be more perfect, the more things the mind understands, and that it will be most perfect when the mind turns itself to the knowledge of the most perfect Being or reflects thereon. Again, the more things the mind knows the better it understands its own powers and the order of nature ; but the better it understands its own powers, so much the more easily can it direct itself and propose rules to itself ; the better also it understands the order of Nature, the more easily can it restrain itself from what is useless. In what we have enumerated consists, as we have said, the whole of the method.

It is also to be observed that it is with the idea objectively as it is with the object of the idea really. If therefore there were anything in Nature which had no connection with other things ; if also its objective essence existed ; since it must altogether agree with its formal essence, this objective essence would have no connection [1] with other ideas, that is to say, we could conclude nothing from it ; on the other hand, those things which are connected with other things, like everything which exists in Nature, will be understood, and their objective essences will have the same connection, that is to say, other ideas will be deduced from them, which again will be connected with others ; and thus instruments for proceeding further will increase. This was what we endeavoured to prove. Moreover, from the last thing we have said, namely, that the idea must altogether agree with its formal essence, it is clear

<hr>

[1] To have connection with other things is to be produced by them or to produce them (*Sp.*).

that in order that our mind may exactly reproduce the pattern of Nature, it must draw all its ideas from that idea which reproduces the origin and fountain of the whole of Nature, so that it may also become the source of other ideas.

Here some may wonder that, since we have said that the good method is that which shows in what manner the mind is to be directed in accordance with the standard of a given true idea, we should prove it by reasoning—a proceeding which seems to show that this statement is not self-evident. It may consequently be asked if our reasoning is valid. If the reasoning is valid, we must begin from a given idea : and since to begin from a given idea needs a demonstration, we must again prove our reasoning ; and that proof must again be proved, and so on *ad infinitum.* But to this I reply that if anybody had been led by good fortune to proceed in this way[1] in the investigation of Nature, that is to say, by acquiring ideas in their proper order according to the standard of a given true idea, he would never have doubted of their truth,[2] because the truth, as we have shown, is self-evident and all things would have flowed spontaneously towards him. But because this never or rarely happens, I have been compelled to explain myself thus, in order that what we cannot acquire by good fortune we may acquire by means of a pre-considered plan ; and that it may appear that in order to test truth and to be

---

[1] *Quod si quis fato quodam sic processisset—i.e.,* by the good method. —TRANS.

[2] Just as here we do not doubt of our truth (*Sp.*), *de nostra veritate*—of the truth of what we maintain to be true. —TRANS.

sure of our reasoning we need no other instruments
than truth itself and good reasoning. For I have
proved reasoning to be good by reasoning well, and
endeavour so to prove it. Besides, this is the way
in which men become accustomed to internal medi-
tations.

The reason why in the investigation of Nature it
rarely happens that it is conducted in the proper
order is because of prejudices, the causes of which
will be afterwards explained in our Philosophy.
Secondly, as we shall afterwards show, there is need
of great and accurate distinction, a thing which is
very laborious. Finally, it is because of the condition of human affairs which, as[1] we have already
shown, is very changeable. There are also other
reasons into which we do not inquire. If anybody
by chance should ask why, as truth is self-evident,
I do not myself before everything set forth the
truths of Nature in that order, I reply with a warn-
ing that because things he may meet with here and
there may seem paradoxical[2] he is not to reject
them as false, but first consider the order in which
we prove them and then he will be certain that we
have reached the truth. This was the reason for
what I have premised. If after this any sceptic

[1] To what Spinoza refers when he says " as we have already
shown " is not clear, unless it is to the dangers attending the
pursuit of wealth (p. 4), nor is it clear why the mutability of
human affairs should be specially mentioned in this connection.
Probably something is omitted in the text as we now have it.—
TRANS.

[2] This passage is not quite intelligible to me. I cannot clearly
see what are the paradoxes to which Spinoza refers. Apparently,
according to the connection of the words, the paradox is that he
has not contented himself with setting forth the truths of Nature
in their proper order.—TRANS.

should still remain doubtful of the primary truth itself and all those things which we shall deduce in accordance with the standard of the primary truth, he will indeed speak contrary to his conviction or we shall confess that there are men who in their minds are utterly blind from birth or through prejudice, that is to say, by some external accident. For they are not self-conscious : if they affirm anything or doubt anything, they know not that they doubt or affirm : they say that they know nothing ; and this very thing itself—that they know nothing—they say they do not know ; nor can they say this absolutely, for so long as they know nothing they are afraid to confess that they exist, so that at last they are reduced to silence lest by chance they should make any supposition which should have any appearance of truth in it. Finally, no one can speak to them about the sciences ; but so far as the custom of life and society is concerned, necessity compels them to suppose that they exist ; to seek that which is useful to them, and to affirm or deny many things on oath. If anything be proved to them, they do not know if the reasoning is valid or defective. If they deny, concede or oppose, they do not know that they deny, concede or oppose ; and thus they must be set down as automata altogether destitute of mind.

We will now return to the subject set before us. We have had before us so far—

(1) The end to which we desire to direct all our thoughts.

(2) We have determined what is the best kind of

5

knowledge whereby we may attain our perfection.

(3) We have determined what is the path which the mind must first pursue, in order that it may begin well—that is to say, it must proceed to make a systematic investigation in accordance with the standard of some existing true idea. In order that it may do this properly, it is the business of Method, in the first place, to distinguish a true idea from all other perceptions, and to restrain the mind from other perceptions ; secondly, to lay down rules whereby unknown things may be perceived in accordance with this standard ; thirdly, to arrange the order so that we shall not be wearied out by that which is useless. After we came to know what the method was, we saw, in the fourth place, that it would be most perfect when we possessed the idea of the most Perfect Being. Therefore, at the beginning, it is to be our chief care that as speedily as possible we attain to the knowledge of such a Being.

Let us begin, therefore, with the first part of Method, which is, as we have said, to distinguish and separate a true idea from other perceptions, and to restrain the mind from confounding false, fanciful,[1] and doubtful ideas with true ideas. I desire to explain this matter here as fully as possible, in order to hold my readers to the consideration of a subject so important ; and also because there are

---

[1] " Fictas." It is difficult to find any one English word which will cover exactly the Latin word and translate it in each passage. Spinoza intends generally that which is figured by the imagination or *phantasied*.—TRANS.

many persons who doubt even what is true, because they have not attended to the distinction between true perception and all others, so that they are as men who, when they are awake, do not doubt that they are awake, but afterwards doubt their waking moments, because once in their dreams, as often happens, they have considered themselves to be of a certainty awake, and have afterwards discovered that this was an error. This happens because they never distinguished between sleeping and waking.

Meantime, I warn my readers that I shall not here explain the essence [1] of each kind of perception, and that through its proximate cause, for this is the province of Philosophy. I shall set forth only what the Method demands—that is to say, with what fanciful, false, and doubtful perception are concerned, and in what manner we can be freed from them. Our first inquiry, therefore, will be about the idea of the imagination.

Since all perception is either of an object considered as existing, or of essence alone, and fancies more frequently occur with regard to objects considered as existing, I will therefore speak of this case first, that is to say, the case in which existence alone is imagined, and the thing which is thus imagined is understood or is supposed to be understood. For example, I imagine that Peter, whom I know, is going home, that he is coming to see me, and the like.[2] Here I ask, with what is this idea concerned? I see that it has to do with things possible only ;

[1] *I.e.*, false, imaginary, and doubtful perception.—TRANS.
[2] See further on what we say concerning hypotheses which

not with those which are necessary or impossible.
I call a thing impossible if its nature implies a contradiction to its existence ; necessary, if its nature
implies a contradiction to its non-existence ; and
possible, if its existence by its very nature does not
involve a contradiction to its existence or to its
non-existence (*cujus quidem existentia, ipsâ suâ
naturâ non implicat contradictionem, ut existat aut
non existat*), the necessity or impossibility of its
existence depending on causes unknown to us, while
we are imagining its existence. If, therefore, its
necessity or impossibility, which depends on external
causes, were known to us, we could imagine nothing
concerning it.   Hence it follows that if any God
or anything omniscient exists, it is impossible for it [1]
to fancy anything with regard to it.   For to take my
own case, after I know [2] that I exist, I cannot fancy
that I do or do not exist : nor can I fancy an elephant
which can pass through the eye of a needle ; nor,
after I know the nature of God,[3] fancy him existing

we clearly understand.   The fiction consists in the assignment
of existence in the celestial bodies to these hypotheses (*Sp.*).

[1] Reading *nihil prorsus hoc posse fingere* after the Dutch
version.—TRANS.

[2] Because the thing, provided only it be understood, is self-
evident ; we need nothing more, therefore, than an example
without any other demonstration.   The same thing is true of its
contrary ; for, in order that it may be evident that it is false, it
is simply necessary that it be examined, as we shall presently
show when we speak of fancy which concerns itself with
essence (*Sp.*).

[3] Observe, although many say that they doubt the existence
of God, they have nothing before them but a name, or, as I
shall afterwards show in the proper place, they picture something
which has no agreement with the nature of God, and call it
God (*Sp.*).

or not existing. The same thing is to be said of
the Chimæra, whose nature implies non-existence.[1]
Hence it is evident, as I have said, that imagination,
of which we now speak, has nothing to do with
eternal truths.[2] Before, however, I proceed further,
it may here be observed, by the way, that whatever
is the difference between the essence of one thing
and that of another, there is the same difference
between the actuality or existence of the one and
the actuality or existence of the other.   Therefore,
if we desire to conceive the existence—say of Adam
—through general existence only, it will be the
same as if, for the purpose of conceiving his essence,
we attend to the nature of being and define Adam
as Being.   Therefore, the more generally existence
is conceived, the more confusedly it is conceived,
and the more easily can it be assigned to any given
thing ; on the other hand, when it is more particularly conceived, it is more clearly understood, and it
is ascribed with more difficulty to anything, unless
it be an object which we conceive without paying

---

[1] *Cujus natura existere implicat.* So in ed. 1677, in Paulus,
Bruder, and in Van Vloten and Land.   So also in Auerbach's
translation.   Saisset's translation is *dont la nature est telle qu'il
implique contradiction qu'elle existe.* It is clear that *non* ought
to be inserted before *existere.* See *Cog., Met.* i. 3 : *Chimæra
vero respectu implicantiæ suæ essentiæ non potis est, ut existat,*
and see also note below.—TRANS.

[2] I shall show immediately that no fancy is concerned with
eternal truths.   By an eternal truth, I understand truth of such
a kind that, if it be affirmative, it can never be negative.   Thus
it is a primary and eternal truth that God is ; but it is not an
eternal truth that Adam thinks.   That a Chimæra is not is an
eternal truth, but it is not an eternal truth that Adam does not
think (*Sp.*).

attention to the order of Nature.[1]   This is worthy
of observation.

Those things are now to be considered which are
commonly said to be imagined, although we clearly
understand that the thing is not as we picture it to
be. For example, although I know the earth is
round, nothing forbids me to tell anybody that it
is a half-globe, like half an orange in a plate, or
that the sun goes round the earth, and other things
of the same kind. If we consider this, we shall see
nothing which is not in accord with what we have
already said.[2]   We must, however, remember that
we have sometimes made mistakes, and now are
conscious of our errors, and that we can imagine,
or at least suppose, that other men are in the same
error, or may fall into it, as we did previously.
This, I say, we can imagine, so long as we see no
impossibility and no necessity ; when, therefore, I
tell anybody that the earth is not round, I simply
recall a former error which I used to believe, or into
which I was apt to fall, and afterwards I imagine or

[1] Whatever may be the difference between the essences of
things, there is a corresponding difference between their actuality
or existence. If, therefore, we consider Adam's existence as
mere general existence, Adam's essence becomes mere Being.
Conceiving, therefore, existence generally, it is conceived confusedly, and is easily attributable, for Being, the corresponding
essence, is very simple.   On the other hand, if we conceive
existence particularly, the difficulty of attribution is increased (*Sp.*).
Such is Spinoza's way of putting it.   We should say that the
more generally we imagine a thing, the easier it is to imagine
its existence.   The more definite a conception is, and the more
relationships it has, the less easy is it to consider it as existing,
or rather the stronger are the reasons which have to be given for
existence.—TRANS.

[2] Namely, that if impossibility depending on external causes be
known to us, we can picture nothing.—TRANS.

suppose that he to whom I speak is still in the same error, or may fall into it. This, as I have said, I imagine, so long as I see no impossibility and no necessity. If I had understood that there was any impossibility or necessity, I could form no fancy, and the only thing I could say would be that I had effected something (*me aliquid operatum esse*).

It remains for us now to note the suppositions made in discussions, even at times when impossibilities are involved. For example, when we say let us suppose that this candle now burning does not burn, or let us suppose that it burns in some imaginary space, or one in which no bodies exist. Things of this sort are often supposed, although the case last mentioned is clearly seen to be an impossibility, but when we make these suppositions, nothing whatever is imagined, for in the first instance [1] I have done nothing more than call to mind another candle not burning (or have imagined the candle before me to be without flame), and what I conceive of that other candle, I attribute to the

---

[1] Afterwards, when we speak of imagination which has to do with essences, it will clearly appear that imagination never creates, nor offers to the mind, any new thing, but that those things only which are in the brain or in the imagination are awakened in the memory, and that the mind confusedly occupies itself with them all simultaneously. For example, speech and a tree are remembered, and the mind looking at them both confusedly, and without distinguishing them, thinks of a tree as speaking. The same thing is to be understood of existence, especially, as we have said, when it is conceived so generally as being, for it is then easily applied to all things which are simultaneously remembered. This is particularly worth observation (*Sp.*).

one before me, so long as I do not attend to the flame. In the second case, I do nothing but abstract my thoughts from surrounding bodies, so that my mind occupies itself with the contemplation of the candle alone considered in itself. In this way I may afterwards conclude that there is no reason in the candle for its own destruction, so that if there were no surrounding bodies, the candle as well as the flame would remain unchangeable. And so with similar suppositions. There is here no imagination, but true and pure assertions.[1]

We now turn to fancies which have to do with essences alone or accompanied by some actuality or existence. Concerning these the main consideration is that the less the mind understands, and the more things it perceives, the greater power of fancying it has, and the more things it understands the more is that power lessened. For example, in the same way as we have just seen that, so long as we think, we cannot fancy that we think and do not think, so also after we know the nature of the body we cannot fancy an infinite fly ; or after we have known the nature of the soul [2] we cannot fancy it

---

[1] This is also true of hypotheses which are formed in order to explain certain motions corresponding to celestial phenomena, provided in applying them to the celestial phenomena, we do not conclude the nature of the heavens, which may be very different, especially as many other causes may be conceived for the explanation of these motions (*Sp.*).

[2] It often happens that a man recalls this word "soul" in his memory and at the same time forms some bodily image. Since these two are simultaneously represented, he easily thinks that he imagines and pictures a corporeal soul, because he does not distinguish the name from the thing itself. Here I ask my readers not to be hasty with refutation. I believe they will not, if they will

four-sided, although we may say anything in words.'
But, as we have said, the less men know nature, so
much the more easily they can fancy many things,
as that trees speak, that men are changed in a
moment into stones or into springs of water, that
ghosts are seen in mirrors, that nothing becomes
something, also that gods are changed into beasts
and men, and an infinite number of other things
of the same kind. Some will perhaps suppose that
fancy and not intelligence limits fancy, that is to
say, having pictured something and having voluntarily of my own accord affirmed that the thing so
exists in nature, I am afterwards unable to conceive
it in any other way. For example, having fancied,
to use their own language, that the body has a
certain nature, and having of my own accord
voluntarily persuaded myself that thus it really
exists, it is no longer possible for me to imagine an
infinite fly ; and having imagined the essence of the
soul, it is no longer possible to fancy that it is four-
sided. Let us examine this theory. In the first
place, they either deny or grant that we can understand something. If they grant it, what they
affirm of fancy they must necessarily affirm of
intelligence.[1] If they deny, let us who know that
we know something see what it is they say. This
is what they say—that the mind can apprehend
and perceive in many ways, not itself, nor things

attend as closely as possible to the examples, and to what follows
(*Sp.*).
    [1] *I.e.*, that having *understood* a thing, conclusions necessarily
follow and the fiction is determined, terminated thereby.—
TRANS.

which exist, but only those which are not in themselves and nowhere exist, that is to say, that the
mind can by its own strength create sensations or
ideas which do not belong to things, so that in a
measure they make it out to be a God. Moreover
they assert that we, or our mind, has such freedom
that it can control us, or itself, and indeed its own
freedom. For after the mind has imagined something, and has yielded assent to it, it cannot think
or picture that thing in any other way, and by that
figment of the imagination it is compelled to think
other things in such a way as may not contradict it.
In this way, they are compelled to admit, on account
of what they have imagined, the absurdities just
mentioned which we will not take the trouble to
refute by any demonstrations.[1] But leaving them
in their delusions, we will take care to draw from
the argument with them some truth suitable to our
purpose — namely this, that the mind, when it
attends to anything merely pictured, and in its

[1] Although I may appear to reason from experience, and it
may be said that what I have asserted is nothing because a
demonstration is not provided, it can be proved as follows for
those who desire proof. Since in Nature there can be nothing
which opposes its laws and since all things happen according to
its certain laws and by them produce their own certain effects in
inviolable order, it follows that the soul when it truly conceives
a thing advances to form objectively those same effects. See
below where I speak of the false idea (*Sp.*).
To understand this note we must remember that to Spinoza,
nature is *formally* what the mind is *objectively*. When, therefore, the mind forms a true idea, an objective process follows
corresponding to the formal process in Nature and true results
are deduced. It is these which limit and abolish fiction. The
reference to the false idea is probably more particularly to the
passage in which it is laid down that a perfectly clear and distinct
idea cannot be false.—TRANS.

nature false, in order to examine and reflect upon it thoroughly and deduce in proper order from it the conclusions which are deducible, will easily lay open the falsity ; and if the thing pictured or imagined be in its nature true, when the mind attends to it, so as to understand it, and begins to deduce from it in proper order the conclusions which thence follow, it will happily advance without any interruption, as we have seen that the intellect immediately proceeded to prove from the false figment of the imagination just cited its absurdity, and the absurdity also of the deductions from it.[1]

There is then no cause for fear that we fancy anything, provided only that we clearly and distinctly perceive the object, for if by chance we say that men in a moment are changed into beasts we speak very generally, so that there is no concept, that is to say, idea or coherence of subject and predicate in the mind, for if there were any, the mind would at once discern the means and the causes through which such an event happened. Neither, again, is attention paid to the nature of the subject and the predicate. But provided the first idea be not fancied and all the other ideas are deduced from it, the impulse to fancy will gradually vanish. Again, since an idea of the imagination cannot be clear and distinct, but is nothing but confusion, and all confusion arises because the mind knows a whole

---

[1] It is not very clear against what particular sophistry this argument is directed. It would have been interesting if Spinoza had referred us to particular authors. He seems to have had in his mind some heresy that a fiction is a fiction merely because it contradicts an assumption which is also a fiction.—TRANS.

or a complex only in part, and does not distinguish the known from the unknown : because also it considers simultaneously without any distinction the many things which are contained in each object, it follows (1) that if the idea be that of an object perfectly simple it can only be clear and distinct. For such a thing cannot be known partially ; it must be known wholly or not at all.   It follows (2) that if a thing which is complex be divided in thought into parts which are each perfectly simple, and we attend to each one separately, all confusion will then disappear.   It follows (3) that a fancy cannot be simple, but that it arises from putting together diverse confused ideas which belong to diverse things and operations in nature, or rather from attending to these diverse ideas without admitting their reality.[1]   If a fancy were simple, it would be clear and distinct and consequently true. If it arose from the composition of distinct ideas, their composite whole would be clear and distinct, and therefore true.   For example, when we know the nature of a circle and also of a square, we cannot possibly compound them and make a square circle or a square soul, and so on.

Again, to conclude briefly, let us see how it is that we need not fear that a fancy can be confounded

---

[1] N.B.—A fancy considered in itself is not very different from a dream, save that in dreams no reasons appear, such as by the help of the senses are presented to persons awake, from which they gather that those appearances at that time are not the representations of things existing outside them.   Error, on the other hand, as will presently appear, is dreaming while we are awake and if it is very obvious is called delusion (*Sp.*)

with true ideas. For taking the fancy of which we
first spoke, that is to say, the case in which a thing
is clearly conceived, we saw that if that thing, which
is clearly conceived, and also the existence of that
thing, be an eternal truth of itself, we cannot fancy
anything about it, but if the existence of the thing
conceived is not an eternal truth, what we have to
do is to take care that the existence of the thing be
compared with its essence, and at the same time
that attention be paid to the order of nature.

With regard to the second action of the imagination, which we have said consists in simultaneous
attention, without assent, to different confused
ideas of different things and operations existing in
nature, we have seen that a perfectly simple thing
cannot be imagined but can be understood, and
that this is also true of a thing which is composite,
provided we attend to the perfectly simple parts
of which it is composed—nay, more, we cannot
imagine any actions of these parts which are not
true, for we shall be compelled to consider in what
manner and why anything so happens.[1]

Having understood so far, let us pass to the
inquiry concerning the false idea, and let us see
how it arises and in what manner we may protect
ourselves from false perceptions. Neither of these
inquiries will now be difficult to us after the inquiry concerning the idea of imagination, for there
is no difference between them, excepting that the

---

[1] We cannot, for example, conceive that a horse flies because
attending to the simple parts—horse and flying—we cannot see
how the two parts can be brought together.—TRANS.

false idea supposes assent to its reality, that is to say, as we have already noted,[1] no reasons appear, when representations are presented to us, from which it can be gathered, as in the case of the idea of the imagination, that the false idea does not arise from objects outside us, and that it is almost the same as dreaming with the eyes open or awake. The false idea, therefore, in the same way as the idea of imagination, is either concerned with, or — to speak more correctly — is related to, the existence of a thing whose essence is known, or with its essence   The false idea which is related to existence is corrected in the same way as a fancy, for if the nature of the known thing supposes necessary existence, it is impossible that we should be deceived as to the existence of that thing ; but if the existence of the thing, unlike its essence, is not an eternal truth, but the necessity or impossibility of its existence depends on external causes, then everything which we have said of fancy applies also in this case, and the correction is the same.   With regard to the other kind of false idea which is related to essences and also to operations, such perceptions are necessarily always confused, composed of different confused perceptions of objects existing in nature, as when men are persuaded that divinities are present in woods, in images, in brutes, and other things, that there are bodies, from the mere composition of which the intellect arises, that corpses can reason, walk, speak, that God is deceived, and the like. But ideas which are clear and distinct can never be false, for the ideas of things which are clearly and distinctly conceived are either perfectly simple or are composed of perfectly simple ideas, that is to say, deduced from them. That a perfectly simple idea cannot be false, everybody can see, provided he knows what true means, or what understanding means, and at the same time what false means.

For as regards what constitutes the form of truth, it is certain that true thought is distinguished from false thought not only by an external but mainly by an internal mark ; as, for example, if a workman has rightly conceived any structure, although the thing has never existed and will never exist, his thought is nevertheless true, and the thought is the same whether the thing exists or not. On the other hand, if any person says that Peter, for example, exists, and does not know that he exists, that thought, so far as that person is concerned, is false, or if it be preferred so to speak, is not true, notwithstanding that Peter may actually exist. Nor is the proposition that Peter exists true excepting for the man who knows certainly that Peter exists. Hence it follows that there is something real in ideas, by which the true are distinguished from the false. This we must now investigate in order that we may have the best standard of truth (for we have said that we must determine our thoughts by the given standard of a true idea, and that the method is knowledge arising from reflection),[1] and

[1] See p. 18.—TRANS.

in order that we may know the properties of the intellect. Nor let it be said that the true idea differs from the false idea because the true thought knows things through their first causes (although the true idea is certainly to be distinguished from the false in this respect, as we have already explained) : [1] for a thought is also said to be true which contains objectively the essence of some principle that has no cause, and is known through and in itself. Therefore the form of true thought must lie in that same thought itself without relation to other thoughts, nor does it acknowledge an object as its cause, but it must depend upon the power itself and nature of the intellect. For if we suppose the intellect to have perceived some new being which had never existed, as some imagine the intellect of God before He created things (a perception which could not possibly arise from any object), and if we also suppose the intellect to deduce other perceptions legitimately from the first, all those thoughts would be true and determined by no external object, but would depend solely on the power and nature of the intellect. Therefore, that which constitutes the form of true thought is to be sought in that same thought itself, and is to be deduced from the nature of the intellect. In order to make this clear, let us place before our eyes some true idea, the object of which we know with perfect certainty depends upon our power of thinking, and has no object in nature : for in such an idea, as is evident from what has already been

[1] See p. 26.—TRANS.

said, we shall more easily discover what we desire' to know. For example, in order to form the concept of a globe, I imagine arbitrarily a cause, that is to say, the revolution of a semi-circle round a centre, and that from the revolution a globe, as it were, is produced. This idea is certainly true, and although we know that no globe was ever so produced in nature, the perception nevertheless is true, and it is the easiest mode of forming a concept of a globe. It is now to be observed that this perception affirms that the semi-circle rotates, an affirmation which would be false, if it were not joined to the concept of a globe, or of a cause producing such a motion, that is to say, it would be absolutely false if the affirmation were a bare affirmation. For in that case the mind would only go so far as to affirm solely the motion of a semi-circle, which is not contained in the concept of a semi-circle, nor arises from the concept of a cause producing the motion. Therefore falsity consists solely in the affirmation concerning anything of something which is not contained in the concept we have formed of the thing, as, for example, in the affirmation of motion and rest of a semi-circle. Hence it follows that simple thoughts cannot be other than true, such, for example, as the simple idea of the semi-circle, of motion, of quantity, &c. Whatever of affirmation these ideas contain is equal to their concept, and does not go beyond this. Wherefore it is permitted to us without any fear of error to form at pleasure simple ideas. It remains, therefore, merely to inquire by what

6

power our mind can form them, and what is the
extent of that power, for when we have discovered
this, we shall easily discern the most perfect knowledge to which we can attain. For it is clear that
the extent of this power of the mind is not infinite.
For when of any object we affirm something which
is not contained in the concept which we form of
that object, a defect in our perception is thereby
indicated so that we have ideas and thoughts which
are mutilated and, as it were, incomplete. For we
have seen that the motion of a semi-circle is false,
as a disconnected affirmation in the mind, but that
it is true if it be joined to the concept of a globe,
or to the concept of any cause determining such
motion.   Moreover if, as is self-evident, it belongs
to the nature of a thinking being to form true or
adequate thoughts, it is certain that inadequate
ideas arise in us solely because we are part of some
thinking being, whose thoughts, some in their com-
pleteness and others in part only, form our mind.[1]

[1] "Hence it follows that the human mind is a part of the
infinite intellect of God, and therefore, when we say that the
human mind perceives this or that thing, we say nothing else
than that God has this or that idea; not indeed in so far as
He is infinite, but in so far as He is manifested through the
nature of the human mind, or in so far as He forms the
essence of the human mind; and when we say that God has
this or that idea, not merely in so far as He forms the nature of
the human mind, but in so far as He has at the same time with
the human mind the idea also of another thing, then we say that
the human mind perceives the thing partially or inadequately "
(*Ethic*, Coroll., Prop. xi., pt. 2).
  "I consider the mind as a part of Nature, because I maintain
that in Nature there is an infinite power of thought, which in
so far as it is infinite, contains in itself all Nature objectively,
and its thoughts proceed in the same manner as Nature, that is

We have, however, here to observe what it was'
not worth while to notice when we were dealing
with imagination, that it is a most fruitful cause
of deception when certain things which are presented to us in the imagination are also in the
intellect, that is to say, are clearly and distinctly
conceived, because then, so long as that which is
distinct is not distinguished from that which is
confused, certitude, that is to say, the true idea,
is mixed with those which are not distinct. For
example, certain of the Stoics had by chance
heard the name of the soul, and also that it is
immortal, and both the soul and immortality
were imagined confusedly : they also imagined
and at the same time understood that bodies
which are most subtle penetrate all others, and
are penetrated by none. The certainty of this
axiom accompanying those things which they
imagined simultaneously, they immediately became assured that the mind is those most subtle
bodies, and that those most subtle bodies cannot
be divided, &c. But from error of this kind we
are set free if we attempt to examine all our
perceptions by the standard of a given true idea,

to say, in that mode of it which is the mode of ideas." [" *Procedunt eodem modo ac Natura, ejus nimirum ideatum*," ed.
1677, and Van Vloten and Land. So also autograph at the
Royal Society Lond. " *Procedunt eodem modo ac Natura ejus,
nimirum idearum*," ed. Paulus. So also Bruder.] " Again I assert
that the human mind possesses this power, not in so far as it is
infinite and perceives the whole of Nature, but in so far as it is
finite, that is to say, in so far only as it perceives the human
body, and in this way I consider the human mind part of a
certain infinite intellect" (Letter to Oldenburg, November 20,
1665).—TRANS.

by being on our guard as we have said at the beginning against the perceptions which we obtain from hearing or from vague experience.

It is to be observed also that deception of the same kind arises from conceiving things too abstractly, for it is self-evident that I cannot apply to another that which I perceive in its own true object. Finally, it arises from not understanding the primary elements of the whole of Nature, so that by proceeding without order and confusing Nature with abstract axioms, although they may be true, we confuse ourselves and pervert the order of Nature.[1] This deception, however, is in no way to be feared if we proceed as little as possible abstractly, and begin as early as possible from primary elements, that is to say, from the fountain and origin of Nature. As to the knowledge of the origin of Nature, there is no fear whatever of confounding it with abstractions, for when a thing is conceived abstractly like all universals, the intellect comprehends more than the particulars actually existing in Nature. Again, since there are many things in Nature with differences so small that they escape the understanding, it may easily happen, if these things are conceived abstractly, that they may be confused one with the other ; but since the origin of Nature, as we shall afterwards see, can be conceived neither abstractly

---

[1] The deception of the Stoics arose from considering the subtlety of body in too abstract a manner. Subtlety ought to be confined to its own proper object—body ; but it was conceived too abstractly and applied to spirit.—TRANS.

nor universally, nor can be extended more widely in the intellect than it is actually, nor has any similitude with mutable things, no confusion with regard to its idea is to be feared provided only we possess the standard of truth, which we have just set forth. For this Being is one [1] and infinite ; it is in fact all being,[2] without which nothing exists.

Thus much concerning the false idea. It remains now to consider the doubtful idea, that is to say, to consider what those things are which lead us to doubt, and in what manner doubt may be removed. I speak now of true doubt in the mind, and not of that doubt not infrequent, when a man affirms in words that he doubts although his mind dces not doubt. This it is not the office of the method to correct ; it appertains rather to an inquiry into obstinacy and its correction. Doubt is never produced in the mind by the object itself concerning which we doubt, that is to say, if there be only a single idea in the mind, whether it be true or false, there is neither doubt nor certitude, but only a certain sensation, for the idea is in itself nothing but this sensation. Doubt is caused by another idea, which is not so clear and distinct that we can deduce from it any certainty concerning the thing of which we doubt, that is

---

[1] These are not attributes of God which set forth His essence, as I shall show in the Philosophy (*Sp.*).

[2] This has already been demonstrated. For if such a Being did not exist, it could never be produced, and so the mind would be able to apprehend more than Nature could supply, which we have already shown to be false (*Sp.*). The demonstration is in the preceding sentence. The argument is that the Origin of Nature cannot be extended more widely in the intellect than it is in Nature.—TRANS.

to say, the idea which causes us to doubt is not clear and distinct. For example, if we have never reflected on the deceptiveness of the senses, whether it arises from experience [1] or in whatever other way, we shall never doubt whether the sun is greater or less than he appears to be. Ignorant people therefore generally wonder when they hear that the sun is much larger than this earthly globe, but by thinking on the deceptiveness of the senses doubt arises,[2] and if after doubt, we acquire a true knowledge of the senses and know in what way by their instrumentality objects are represented at a distance, doubt is again removed. Hence it follows that we cannot doubt true ideas on the supposition that some deceiving God exists who deceives us even in things most certain, except so long as we have no clear and distinct idea ; that is to say, so long as we reflect upon the knowledge we have of the source of all things, without discovering anything which teaches us as certainly that He does not deceive, as we know, when we consider the nature of a triangle, that its three angles are equal to two right angles. If, however, we have such a knowledge of God as we have of a triangle, then all doubt is removed. And by the same manner by which we can arrive at such a knowledge of the triangle, although we do not certainly know whether a supreme deceiver may

---

[1] That is to say, as a mistaken inference from what the senses report.—TRANS.

[2] That is to say it is known that the senses are sometimes deceived, but it is only known confusedly. It is not known in what manner they deceive (*Sp.*).

not deceive us, we can also arrive at such a
knowledge of God although we do not certainly
know whether any supreme deceiver exists; and
provided we have that knowledge, it will be
sufficient, as I have said, to remove all doubt which
we may have concerning clear and distinct ideas.[1]

But if we proceed properly by investigating
those things which are first to be investigated,
without disturbing the sequence of things, and if
we know in what manner questions are to be
determined before we attempt the knowledge of
them, we shall never have any ideas excepting
those which are most certain, that is to say, those
which are clear and distinct. For doubt is nothing
but the suspension of the mind about something
which we would affirm or deny did not something
else interpose, our ignorance of which causes our
knowledge of the thing to be imperfect. Hence it
is to be concluded that doubt always arises because
things are investigated without order.

This is what I promised to treat of in the first
part of the Method. But in order that I may omit
nothing which may conduce to a knowledge of the

[1] This is a difficulty taken over by Spinoza from Descartes.
It is more fully discussed by Spinoza in the Principia, pt. i.
The passage is obscure, but the meaning seems to be that it is
possible to have as clear a knowledge of God as we have of a
triangle, and that, when we have this knowledge we cannot
conceive Him as a deceiver, and consequently the belief in Him
as a deceiver cannot be a reason for doubting true ideas. No
man can doubt that the three angles of a triangle are equal to
two right angles, whatever theory he may form as to a deceiving God. In effect Spinoza protests, as he has protested before,
against getting behind the clear and true idea and the conclusions
therefrom.—TRANS.

intellect and its powers, I will add a few words on memory and forgetfulness. Upon this point the principal thing to be considered is that the memory is strengthened by the help of the understanding and also without its help. For, in the first case, the more easily a thing is understood, the more easily it is retained ; and on the other hand, the less easily it is understood, the more easily we forget it. If, for example, I put before anybody a number of disconnected words, he will recollect them with much greater difficulty than if they were in the form of a story. The memory is also strengthened without the assistance of the understanding, that is to say, by the impression which is made on the imagination or the sense which is called common [1] by some individual corporeal object. I say *individual*, for the imagination is affected by individuals only. If we read, for instance, only one love story, we recollect it perfectly, so long as we do not read more of the same kind, for in that case this one alone takes possession of the imagination, but if there are more of the same kind we imagine them all together, and they are easily confused. I say also corporeal, for the imagination is affected by bodies only. Since therefore the memory is strengthened by the understanding, and also without the understanding, it is to be concluded that it is something diverse from the intellect, and that so far as the intellect is concerned, considered in itself, there is no such thing as memory nor for-

[1] By the sense which is called common Spinoza intends the receptiveness which is common to all the senses.—TRANS.

getfulness. What, then, is memory ? It is nothing
else than the sensation of impressions on the brain
accompanied with attention to the definite duration
of the sensation.[1] This is also shown by recollection. For in the case of recollection the mind
thinks of that sensation but without regard to its continuous duration, and so the idea of that sensation
is not the duration itself of the sensation, that is to
say, the memory itself. Whether ideas themselves
are subject to any decay we shall see in the Philosophy. If this should appear very ridiculous, it is
sufficient for the end we have in view to remember
that in proportion as a thing is more singular is it
the more easily retained, as is evident from the example just mentioned of the comedy. Moreover, in
proportion as a thing is more intelligible is it the
more easily retained. Hence we are unable to
forget a thing absolutely singular if it is intelligible.

Thus, then, we have distinguished between the
true idea and other perceptions, and we have shown
that fancied, false, and other ideas derive their origin
from the imagination, that is to say, from certain
fortuitous (if I may so speak) and disconnected
sensations, which do not arise from the power itself
of the mind, but from external causes, as the body
in dreams or awake is impressed by different kinds

[1] If the duration is indefinite, the recollection of the object is
imperfect, as we are taught by nature. For in order to believe
more vividly what is told us, we ask when and where it happened. For although the ideas themselves have their own
duration in the mind, yet since we are accustomed to determine
duration by the assistance of some measure of movement—this
we do by the help of imagination—we preserve no memory of
anything purely mental (*Sp.*).

of motion. Or, if we like, we can understand by the imagination what we please, provided only it be something different from the intellect, something by means of which the mind is placed in a passive relation. It is all the same whatever we take it to be, so long as we know it to be something vague which reduces the mind to passivity, and so long as we are aware how we are liberated from it by the help of the intellect. Let nobody therefore be surprised that I do not here demonstrate that bodies and other necessary things exist, notwithstanding I speak concerning the imagination, concerning the body and its constitution ; for, as I have said, it is all the same, whatever we take the imagination to be, so long as we know it to be something vague, &c.

We have shown that the true idea is simple or composed of ideas which are simple, and that it shows in what manner and why anything is or has happened,[1] and that its objective effects in the mind proceed according to the formal relations of the object itself.[2] This is the same thing as what the ancients said—namely, that true science proceeds from the cause to the effects—but they have never conceived, so far as I know, as we do here, that the mind acts according to certain laws, and as if, so to

---

[1] See p. 35.—TRANS.

[2] The effects of the idea follow the order of the object in nature, or, in other words, our ideas are those of nature. " The order and connection of ideas is the same as the order and connection of things " (*Ethic*, Prop. vii. pt. 2). Spinoza's doctrine is that the mind is not a tablet upon which objects are simply impressed. Thought and extension are attributes of the one substance and man as a soul is part of the infinite thought which is the spiritual counterpart of the extended universe.—TRANS.

speak, it were a sort of spiritual automaton. Hence, as far as was possible at the outset, we have gained a knowledge of our intellect, and such a standard of true ideas that we need not now fear lest we should confound the true with false or fancied ideas, nor shall we wonder why we understand certain things which are in no way compassed by the imagination, and why there are others in the imagination which are altogether opposed to the understanding ; others, again, which are in harmony with it. For we know that those operations by which imaginations are produced happen according to other laws entirely different from the laws of the intellect, and that the mind has, with regard to the imagination, only a passive relation. Hence it is evident how easily those persons who do not accurately distinguish between the imagination and the intellect may fall into great errors. Such, for example, as that extension must be in a certain place, that it must be finite, that its parts must be really distinguished one from the other, that it is the first and sole foundation of all things, that at a given time it occupies more space than at another, and many other things of the same kind, all of which are entirely opposed to the truth, as we shall show at the proper opportunity.

Again, since words are a part of the imagination, that is to say, we form many conceptions according to the manner in which words are loosely combined in the memory from some disposition of the body, it therefore is not to be doubted that words equally with the imagination, unless we are assiduously on

our guard against them, may be the cause of many
great errors. It is to be noted also that they are
formed according to the caprice and notions of the
vulgar, so that they are nothing but signs of things
as they exist in the imagination, and not as they
exist in the intellect. This is clearly evident from
the fact that to those things which exist only in the
intellect and not in the imagination men have
given most frequently negative names, such as
incorporeal, infinite, &c., and that they express
negatively many ideas which are really affirmative
and *vice versâ*, as, for example, increate, independent, infinite, immortal, &c., because the contraries
of these are much more easily imagined, and therefore first presented themselves to primitive man, and
appropriated the positive names. We affirm and
deny much because the nature of words and not the
nature of things permits us to affirm and deny it,
and so long therefore as we are ignorant of this,
we easily take something which is false to be
true.

We avoid moreover another great cause of
confusion, and one which prevents the intellect
from reflecting on itself. For if we fail to distinguish between the imagination and the intellect
we think that those things which we more easily
imagine are clearer to us, and what we imagine
we think we understand. Hence we put in the
foremost place those things which should be put
last, and thus the true order of advance is per-
verted and nothing is legitimately concluded.

But in order that we may now come to the second

part [1] of this method, I will set forth our object therein, and then the means by which we may attain it. The object therefore is to have clear and distinct ideas, that is to say, such as are formed purely by the mind, and not by fortuitous movements of the body. Again, in order to reduce all our ideas to one, we shall endeavour to connect and arrange them in such a way that our mind, as much as possible, may reproduce objectively the actual order of nature both with reference to the whole and to its parts.

With regard, then, to the first point, as we have already set forth, our ultimate object requires that a thing should be conceived either through its essence alone, or through its proximate cause. If the thing is in itself, or as is commonly said, self-caused, it must then be understood through its essence alone, but if the thing is not in itself, but requires a cause for its existence, it must then be understood through its proximate cause, for in truth [2] the knowledge of the effect is nothing else than the acquisition of a more perfect knowledge of

---

[1] The principal rule of this part, as follows from the first part, is to review all the ideas which we discover belong purely to the mind in us, in order that they may be distinguished from those which we imagine. This distinction we shall elicit from the properties of each, that is to say, of the imagination and the intellect (*Sp.*).

The object of the second part (p. 24), is " to lay down rules whereby unknown things may be perceived in accordance with this standard " (the standard of the true idea).—TRANS.

[2] Observe that hence it is apparent that we can understand nothing of nature without at the same time making our knowledge of the first cause, that is to say, of God, more ample. (*Quin simul cognitionem primæ causæ, sive Dei, ampliorem reddamus*) (*Sp.*).

the cause. Hence it will never be permitted to us
so long as we are engaged upon our inquiry into
the nature of things, to conclude anything from
abstract conceptions, and we must above everything take care not to confound what is merely in
the intellect with what is in the thing. But the
best conclusion will be drawn from some particular
affirmative essence, or from a true and legitimate
definition. For from universal axioms alone the
mind cannot descend to individuals, since axioms
embrace an infinite number of individuals, and do not
determine the intellect to contemplate one rather
than another. Therefore the right path of discovery
is to form our thoughts from some given definition.
This will be effected the more happily and the
more easily the better we define any object. The
whole of the second part therefore turns upon the
assignment of the conditions of a good definition,
and secondly upon the mode of discovering good
definitions. In the first place we will consider the
conditions of definition.

A definition, if it is to be called perfect, must
explain the innermost essence of the thing, and not
assume in place of it certain properties. To explain
what I mean, omitting other instances, lest I should
seem desirous of disclosing the errors of others, I
will adduce one example of an abstract object which
is not affected by the mode of definition ; that is to
say, the case of a circle. If it be defined to be a
figure of such a nature that lines drawn from its
centre to its circumference are equal, every one sees
that such a definition by no means explains the

essence of a circle, but only a certain property of it. And although, as I have said, with figures and other entities of reason, this is of little consequence, it is of much consequence when we have to do with physical entities and realities, for the properties of things are not understood so long as their essences are unknown, and if these escape us we necessarily pervert that sequence in the intellect which ought to reproduce the sequence in Nature, and we go altogether astray from the end we have in view. In order that we may avoid this fault the following conditions are to be observed in a definition.

I. If the thing be something created, the definition must, as we said, include the proximate cause. For example, a circle according to this rule would be defined as a figure which is described by any line of which one extremity is fixed and the other movable. This definition clearly includes the proximate cause.

II. A conception or definition of a thing is required such that all the properties of the thing, when the definition is considered by itself alone and not conjoined with others, may be inferred from it, as we observe is the case with the definition of the circle. For therefrom it is clearly to be inferred that all lines drawn from the centre to the circumference are equal. That this is a necessary condition of a definition, is so plain to any one who will consider, that it does not seem worth while to stay to demonstrate it, nor to show from this second condition that every definition must be affirmative. I speak of mental affirmation, taking no account of verbal affirmation, which on account of the poverty of language may perhaps be sometimes negatively expressed, although it is understood affirmatively. The essentials of the definition of a thing increate are these :—

I. That it should exclude every cause, that is to say, that the object should need for its explanation no other object save its own being.

II. Given the definition of the thing, there should be no possibility of questioning whether it exists.

III. It should contain no substantives, so far as the mind is concerned (*ut nulla quoad mentem habeat substantiva*),[1] which can be used as adjectives, that is to say, it should not be explained by any abstractions.

IV. Lastly, although this is hardly necessary to note, it is requisite that we should be able to deduce all the properties of the object from its definition. All this becomes plain to anybody who will accurately consider it.

I have also said that the best conclusion will be drawn from some particular affirmative essence. For the more special an idea is, so much the more distinct and therefore so much the clearer it is. Hence the knowledge of particulars is above everything to be sought for by us.

With regard to order,[2] it is necessary for the purpose of arranging and correcting all our perceptions to inquire as soon as possible (and reason

[1] The *quoad mentem* refers to the contrast between mental and verbal affirmation.—TRANS.

[2] This seems to be the beginning of the third section of the second part of the Method—see p. 24.—TRANS.

demands it) whether any Being exists, and at the same time what kind of Being, which is the cause of all things, so that its objective essence may be the cause of all our ideas, and then will our mind, as we have said, as completely as possible, reproduce Nature, for it will possess objectively its essence, its order, and its union. Hence we may see that it is above everything necessary for us to deduce all our ideas from things physical or from real entities, by advancing as strictly as possible according to the sequence of causes from one real entity to another real entity, and not passing over to abstracts and universals, neither for the sake of deducing anything real from them, nor of deducing them from anything real, for in either way we interrupt the true progress of the intellect. It is to be observed, however, that I do not here understand by the sequence of causes and real entities the sequence of individual mutable things, but the sequence only of things fixed and eternal. For to human weakness it would be impossible to compass the sequence of individual mutable things, both because their multitude surpasses all number, and because of the infinite unessential properties in one and the same thing, any one of which may be the cause of the existence or non-existence of the thing, for the existence of individual mutable things has no connection with their essence, or, as we have already said, is not an eternal truth. Moreover it is not necessary that we should understand their sequence, since the essences of individual mutable things are not to be drawn from their sequence or order of

existence, for this gives us nothing but external
marks, relations, or at the best, unessential properties, all of which are far from being the internal
essence of things. This is to be sought from fixed
and eternal things only, and also from the laws
inscribed in them, as it were in true codes, according
to which all individual things are produced and are
ordered. It may indeed be said that these individual mutable things so intimately and essentially,
if I may so speak, depend upon those that are fixed
that the former without the latter can neither be
nor be conceived. Hence these fixed and eternal
things, although they may be singular, nevertheless, on account of their presence everywhere and
their extensive power, will be like universals to us,
or, so to speak, the *genera* of the definitions of
individual mutable things, and proximate causes of
all things.

But since this is so, it seems to be by no means
easy to arrive at a knowledge of these individual
things, for to conceive all things simultaneously is
a work far beyond the strength of the human
intellect, while the order in which one is to be
understood before the other, as we have said, is not
to be sought from their sequence of existence, nor
even from eternal things, for in that region (*ibi*) all
these individual things are in nature simultaneous.
Hence other helps are necessarily to be sought, in
addition to those of which we make use, in order to
understand eternal things and their laws ; but this
is not the place in which to set them forth, nor is it
worth while to do so until we have acquired a

sufficient knowledge of eternal things and their infallible laws, and until the nature of our senses has been made plain to us.

Before we attempt a knowledge of individual things, it will be fitting to set forth those helps which will all of them assist us to know how to use our senses, and to conduct in order and by certain laws the experiments necessary to settle anything under investigation, so that we may conclude from them according to what laws of the eternal things the thing originates, and that its inner nature may be revealed to us, as I shall show in its proper place.[1] Here, to return to the subject before me, I shall merely endeavour to set forth those things which seem necessary in order that we may arrive at a knowledge of eternal things, and may form their definitions in accordance with the conditions already laid down.

To this end it is necessary to call to mind what we have already said, namely, that when the mind dwells upon any thought in order to investigate it, and to deduce in proper order therefrom the legitimate conclusions, it will detect the falsity of the thought if it be false. If, however, it be true, the mind will easily proceed to deduce without any interruption things which are true. This [2] is necessary for our purpose, for when our thoughts set out from no basis of certainty they may come to stop [3]

[1] There is nothing on this subject in the present treatise.— TRANS.

[2] That is to say, a true thought.—TRANS.

[3] The Latin is obscure, but the translation given is in harmony with the context. As an example of the courage with which

(*nam ex nullo fundamento cogitationes nostræ terminari queunt*), and if therefore we desire to investigate the first of all things it is necessary that there should be some basis from which our thoughts may be conducted thither, and since our method is nothing but knowledge arising from reflection, this basis by which our thoughts are conducted can be nothing else than a knowledge of that which constitutes the form of truth and a knowledge of the intellect and its properties and powers, for when we have acquired this knowledge, we have a basis from which we can deduce our thoughts, and a way by which the intellect so far as its capacity permits can arrive at the knowledge of eternal things, with due regard to its powers.

Now, it pertains to the nature of thought to form true ideas, as we have shown in the first part, so we must here inquire what we understand by the strength and power of the intellect. But since the principal part of our method is to understand as completely as possible the powers of the intellect and its nature, we are necessarily compelled (by reason of that which I have set forth in this second part of the method) to deduce this knowledge from the mere definition of thought and intellect. But up to this point we have had no rules for the discovery of definitions, and because we cannot propound them, unless the nature of the intellect or its definition and power be known, it follows that the

translators seek to escape from difficulties, a German translation of this passage may be given—*wo keine grundlage ist, da können unsere gedanken nicht bestimmt werden.*—TRANS.

definition of the intellect must be clear of itself, or that we can understand nothing. The definition, however, is not clear entirely of itself ; but because the properties of the intellect, like all things which we derive from the intellect, cannot be clearly and distinctly perceived unless their nature be known, the definition of the intellect will become plain of itself if we look to those properties of the intellect which we clearly and distinctly understand.[1] We will therefore here enumerate the properties of the intellect, and thoroughly examine them, and make a beginning with the discussion of our innate instruments.[2]

The properties of the intellect which I have specially noted and clearly understand are these.

I. That it involves certitude, that is to say, it knows that things are formally as they are contained in it objectively.

II. That it perceives some things, or forms some ideas directly, independently, and some mediately from other ideas. For example, it forms the idea of quantity independently, and not by attending to other thoughts, but it forms the ideas of motion only by attending to the idea of quantity.

III. The ideas which it forms independently express infinity, but finite ideas it forms from

---

[1] The Latin, which is rather confused, is—" Attamen quia ejus proprietates ut omnia, quæ ex intellectu habemus, clare et distincte percipi nequeunt nisi cognita earum natura, ergo definitio intellectus per se innotescet, si ad ejus proprietates, quas clare et distincte intelligimus attendamus." The last part of the sentence, however, is clear.—TRANS.

[2] See p. 14, *et seq.* (*Sp.*).

others. For, as regards the idea of quantity, if the intellect perceives it through a cause [1] it limits quantity, as, for example, when it perceives that a solid arises from the movement of a plane, a plane from the movement of a line, and a line from the movement of a point. These perceptions do not serve to make us understand, but merely to limit quantity. This is evident because we conceive them arising as it were from motion, and motion nevertheless is not perceived unless quantity is perceived. Furthermore we can continue motion so as to produce a line to infinity. This we could by no means do, if we had not the idea of infinite quantity.

IV. The intellect forms positive ideas before those which are negative.

V. It perceives things not so much under duration as under a certain form of eternity and in infinite number; or rather, in order to perceive things, it attends neither to number nor duration ; but when it imagines things, it perceives them as being of a certain number, limited duration, and quantity.

VI. The clear and distinct ideas which we form seem to follow so entirely from the necessity of our nature, as to depend absolutely on our power alone :

---

[1] *I.e.*, mediately, and not independently through itself. The Latin is *Ideam enim quantitatis, si eam per causam percipit, tum quantitatem determinat.* The Dutch version reads *si per causam percipit, tum eam per quantitatem.* Auerbach and Saisset substitute *idea* for *ideam*, but without any external authority. Kirchmann translates *wenn der verstand nämlich die vorstellung der grösse durch eine ursache erhält, so bestimmt er die grösse,* which confirms the version given above.—TRANS.

but the contrary is the case with confused ideas, for they are often formed without our consent.

VII. The mind can determine in many ways the ideas of things which it forms from other things. For example, in order to describe an elliptical plane it imagines that a pencil in contact with a string is moved round two centres, or it conceives an infinite number of points which always preserve one and the same relation to some given straight line, or it conceives a cone cut by a plane obliquely so that the angle of inclination is greater than the angle at the apex of the cone, and so on in an infinite number of other ways.

VIII. Ideas are more perfect in proportion to the perfection of the object which they express. We do not so much wonder at the artificer who has designed some shrine as at the man who has designed some beautiful temple.

I do not pause to consider other things, such as love, joy, &c., which are related to thought, for they have nothing to do with our present purpose, nor can they be conceived unless the intellect be perceived,[1] for if we take away perception, everything else is taken away. False ideas and ideas of the imagination have nothing positive (as we have shown abundantly), by reason of which they are called false or imaginary, but they are considered as such solely through defect of our knowledge. False and imaginary ideas therefore, as such, can teach us nothing of the essence of thought. This

---

[1] So in original—*nisi percepto intel'ectu.*—TRANS.

is to be sought in those positive properties just enumerated, that is to say, we must establish some common principle, from which these properties necessarily follow, so that if it be granted, they also follow necessarily, and if it be cancelled all of them disappear.

[*The rest is wanting.*]

UNWIN BROTHERS, THE GRESHAM PRESS, CHILWORTH AND LONDON.

www.ingramcontent.com/pod-product-compliance
Lightning Source LLC
Chambersburg PA
CBHW022014050726
47499CB00007BA/2581